NINE HOURS 'TILL SUNRISE

#10 of 10

ORIGINAL AUTHOR COPY

Evrj'14

JUST WATCH OUT!

Better Hero Army

ISBN 1-492-74947-8
ISBN-13 978-1492749479

First Printing: November, 2013
10 9 8 7 6 5 4 3 2 1

Cover design by Kendall Roderick
Cover copyright © 2013 by Evan Ramspott

For Nevada…
…no, wait, for Zombies *from* Nevada

One

Dust swirled and rolled sidelong off the trail as the horses dragged their hooves, heads hung low. The setting sun was at their back, making the bare patches of earth glow like copper. Sagebrush choked the wide desert surrounding the bluff and tiny town ahead. Ben licked his lips and squinted at the sight of a dozen wooden buildings leaning against the hillside. About a quarter mile farther off there were a few toppled canvas tents where a campsite had recently been cleared – or maybe destroyed.

"Why-yute," Jake said, reading the town marker slowly, squinting at the letters. Jake was a teen-aged kid, scrawny compared with the others because he hadn't started filling out yet.

"Woyute," Randy corrected him. Randy was the oldest of the bunch. "It's some kind of Indian word."

"That's what I said," Jake replied irritably. "Why-yute."

"Quiet," Ben said over his shoulder at

the pair of them. Ben was the leader of the gang, so usually the others listened when he gave an order. He had the physical size and stature of a leader too, with his broad shoulders, muscular build, and thick neck. "Ain't nobody around."

"Maybe Pat seen us coming," Jake replied, drawing his rifle from his saddle. The others behind him did likewise. "Got the whole town against us."

Ben didn't disagree, drawing his pistol and looking around toward the bluff above the town.

"If they're thinking of an ambush, they picked the wrong place for it," Ben said, waving his pistol at the cliff top. Anyone up there would be blinded by the setting sun, giving Ben and his band of tired horsemen the upper hand. "Let's ride around behind the buildings. You three that way. Randy, you and Jake with me."

With weapons drawn they coaxed their tired horses around the back sides of the buildings, holding rifles and pistols toward the windows, noticing some were broken out like there had been a gun fight. It worried Ben more than he let on. Randy was his usual calm self, his eyes darting everywhere, soaking things up, but not saying a word or letting on he was scared. Maybe it was his age that gave him such a steady hand. The silver in Randy's beard and hair was a mark of experience even if his pot belly hinted of laziness. Jake, like the other boys they'd split up from, was nervous. Well, that probably wasn't true. Tucker wouldn't be concerned. He liked the notion of being in charge of something, even if it was just Mitch and the Mexican.

"This don't make sense," Randy said quietly. He scratched at his salt and pepper beard with the tip of his pistol. "There's still a couple wagons over there. No horses, no dogs, no sheep or cattle. Where the hell did everyone go?"

"Keep going," Ben said while dismounting.

"Where are you heading?"

"To the saloon," Ben replied, pointing it out between two buildings. From his vantage point, Ben could see a trail of something heavy that had been hauled through the alley toward the wooden walkway outside of the saloon. "Go get the horses some water and fetch the boys. Meet me in there."

"What if there's trouble?" Jake asked excitedly. He had a young face to match the impetuous tone in his voice, hardly man enough to grow a day's worth of stubble in the four days they'd been on the trail.

"Well then I'll do a lot of shooting to

let you all know about it," Ben replied, sliding his pistol back into its holster. "Go on."

Jake wanted to argue, but Randy tossed the reins of Ben's horse at him.

"You heard him," Randy said, coaxing his own horse to keep moving. Jake cursed under his breath but followed Randy as Ben made his way into the alley. Ben approached an open door on the side of the building. Dark stains covered the floor beneath the doorway and over the two steps. He knew somebody had been dragged out, probably bloody and beaten, or dead, and then hauled over to the saloon. The foot prints around the trough in the dirt looked awkward, as though whomever was doing the hauling had been struggling too.

"Hello?" Ben called into the half open door, pushing it aside gently. Inside was a kitchen turned upside down, the table broken, the clapboards pulled sideways and hanging half off the wall, empty. Pretty much everything littering the floor was broken. He didn't go in. Instead, he followed the trail toward the saloon.

Ben looked up and down the street as he crossed. Nothing in either direction. Aside from a brief gust of evening breeze hitting his ear just right, there wasn't a sound anywhere.

"Hello," Ben called while stepping through the open door of the saloon.

"Oh, please, dear God!" a woman said frantically. Ben whipped out his pistol. "Over here!" she called urgently. "Please!"

The interior of the saloon was so dark Ben couldn't make out anything but the general lay of it. There were several large floor-to-ceiling beams holding up the roof and its supports. The bar was off to his right, beneath a second floor of rooms, its stairway collapsed below the first landing. The floor was littered with overturned or broken tables and chairs. The candle chandelier dangled sideways in the center of the room like a rope swing wheel.

"Hello?" Ben asked, searching for the woman who had called out.

"Here!" the woman said desperately and Ben turned his head toward her voice. "Over here, please!"

As his eyes continued to adjust he saw her against one of the beams, her head moving as she spoke. She was on the other side of the beam as if trying to hide from him.

"Please, there's not much time!"

Ben took a few steps closer to discover she was tied to the post, her and another, smaller person beside her. He rushed to the door. "Fellas!" he called. "There's someone in here. Bring some lanterns to see with." He holstered his pistol while hurrying to the woman. "Ma'am, I'll have you free in a minute," he told her, fighting to unsheathe his knife.

"Thank you," she gasped. "Please, cut her out first. My daughter. Save her."

"Ma'am, I'll save you both, just settle down."

"You don't understand," she breathed with terror. "They're coming. I heard 'em!"

"Likely, you just heard me and my boys riding into town is all. There," he said, slicing free the last rope entangling the woman's wrists.

"Hurry!" She struggled with the ropes binding her waist. To the girl she said "it'll be alright, Suzanna." She put a hand to the girl's cheek, brushing aside hair. The girl stared up at her mother.

Ben heard a deep moan.

"It's alright," he said to the girl, thinking it may have been her. "Don't flinch none. I don't want to cut you any."

"Ben?" Randy asked from the door, carrying a lit lantern.

"Hurry!" the woman said frantically, pulling at several ropes still holding her daughter.

"Be careful," Ben snarled. "I've got a knife here!"

"They're almost here," the woman

gasped, wildly yanking on the ropes.

"Who?" Randy asked, plucking his pistol out of its holster. He spun around once, his pistol leading the way, letting the lantern light reach every corner of the emptiness. The light helped Ben figure out the last ropes and he sliced through them to free the little girl.

Mitch spat onto the sidewalk before coming inside. He worked a wad of chewing tobacco in his mouth, looking around with his lantern held high, appraising the destruction. Mitch was a thin, blond man in his twenties, the kind to catch a ladies eye wherever he went, and the kind normally found sitting behind a desk somewhere instead of out on the range.

"What in tarnation?" Mitch asked, and as he did there came another moan, this one louder and closer, as though someone in the room had uttered it.

"Oh, God," the woman said, clutching her daughter Suzanna against her belly. "Get to the rooftops," she insisted and started leading the girl away from Ben.

"Ma'am, wait," Ben said, slipping his knife back into its sheath. "What was that?"

"There's no time!" she insisted as she reached the collapsed stairs. The first six feet of the stairwell had been broken off, on purpose by the looks of it, knocked out with an axe that still lay on the ground beneath it. The woman picked up her daughter and helped her up onto the landing above, then started dragging an overturned chair to help herself. The dragging was accompanied by a low and unsettling echo of yet another moan.

"What was that?" Randy asked. "Ghosts?"

"Worse," the woman said as she hiked up her dress and used the chair against the wall to fling herself up onto the landing, displaying her undergarments in the process.

The moaning continued, almost ceaseless now. It wasn't just one voice.

"Hey," the Mexican, the man they knew as Baha, called from the door of the saloon. He stopped suddenly at hearing the moaning. "¿Qué demonios?" he asked, kissing one of the tokens from a necklace of dried ears he wore around his neck. His big frame and sombrero eclipsed what little sunlight was stretching into the room.

There was a loud snap of wood from behind the bar like some trap door being dropped to the ground. With it the moaning doubled. The Mexican cranked his repeating rifle, whispering an oath.

"Get to the roof tops!" the woman hollered over the sound. She pushed her daughter up to the top of the stairs.

A head swayed back and forth from

behind the bar, rising slowly out of the shadows of the lantern light like somebody coming up stairs. The man's mouth was gaping open and bellowing low, wanton moans. Then another head appeared behind his, so close the two men stumbled over each other slightly, then came another head.

"Hello?" Ben called out and the moaning men turned their gaze toward him, sunken, haunting eyes that widened grotesquely at seeing Ben and Randy.

"Stop there," Randy warned, holding up his pistol.

"Run!" the woman called out one last time before disappearing through a door on the second floor.

"He said stop!" Mitch called out, raising his pistol and aiming it at the man in front. More men, and now a woman, were appearing in that same, slow, shuffling manner, rising from the depths of the earth through some gateway behind the bar. "We ain't telling you again!"

"Mitch," Ben said, raising a hand to get his attention. He didn't want the kind of senseless bloodshed Mitch was occasioned to do. "Folks," Ben went on, addressing the growing crowd of moaning and advancing people. "Just stop where you are! We don't want to hurt none of you."

More men and women continued to spill out, forming a line coming around the bar, shuffling directly toward Ben and the others. It was a chilling sight. Aside from sunken faces, several had gaping wounds on their heads, faces, necks, and arms. Dark, dried blood stains covered their torn and ripped clothing.

"Back up," Ben warned Randy, taking his own cautious steps back to where Mitch and Baha stood at the doorway.

"Ben!" Tucker called as he reached the door to the saloon. He leaned in, his shoulder length black hair visible under his hat. "There's people coming out of the hills!"

"Shoot, who are they?" Jake yelled as he appeared beside Tucker. "And who are *they*!?"

"I dunno," Ben called back, then looked back at the kid. "Why ain't you with the horses?"

"They all spooked and ran off," Jake replied emphatically. He looked like a schoolboy being chided for breaking a window. "I couldn't hold all six of them myself. Your damned bitch mare reared up and just about broke my arm!"

Tucker glared at Jake, shaking his head in disdain. Four days of being on the road gave his dark presence the added weight of a nearly grown-in, black beard. Tucker looked back in the saloon, plucking his pistol out of its holster and stepping inside.

"You folks stop!" Mitch said, stepping down in front of Ben and leveling his pistol at the first moaning man. The man's skin looked gray in the lamplight, his hair greasy and moist like he had been down sleeping in the earth a long time. The man took another step forward and Mitch pulled his trigger. Everyone jumped with a start. The man reeled backward from the impact, blood spurting from his chest where he'd been shot. He fell into the other moaners and they followed him down with their senseless eyes. They didn't watch with horror as Ben did, nor with some grim entertained pleasure as some in his gang of men, but instead with a curiosity not unlike a child's at seeing something new. The man slumped to the ground and there was silence as even the moaning ceased.

"That's right!" Mitch told the crowd, waving his gun. "Any more of you come any closer and you'll get the same!"

Ben counted at least twenty in the crowd and looked sidelong at Randy. Randy had a look of concern too, the creases around his eyes softened by his wide-eyed expression. Ben had never seen Randy worried. It made his gray hairs stand out all the more. Something was wrong with all these people. Not one among them seemed to have any sense.

The dead man stirred, his eyes still open. Even Mitch took a step back as the man he had just shot sat up stiffly and rolled over onto his hands and knees, rising again to his feet.

"That ain't possible," Mitch said, pointing his pistol at the rising man. "I shot you!" Mitch shook his pistol angrily at him. The man opened his mouth, rasping a bubbly, gurgling moan. The rest of what Ben assumed were the townsfolk chimed in. *Blam!* Mitch fired his pistol again, hitting the man he'd already shot one more time, dead center in the chest, inches from where he had shot him previously. The man stumbled backwards and was shoved aside by the two men immediately behind. *Blam!* Mitch fired again, this time at the next advancing townsperson, who careened sideways, only to be replaced with the next person from behind. Baha fired his rifle several times into the crowd, knocking three or four people over.

"Get out!" Ben told everyone. "Mitch, come on," he said, tugging at Mitch's arm. Mitch spent the last bullet in his six shooter and fell back, his eyes wide in terror as he saw several of the people he'd already shot stumbling back onto their hands and knees, trying to join in the advancing mob.

Ben and his gang spilled out onto the street, looking both ways for a place to hole up and defend.

"Get on the rooftops!" the woman yelled down at them. "You can't stop 'em. What are you waiting for? Come on! Get up!"

"There," Randy said, pointing out an awning post next to a hitching post. Randy put down his lantern and started to climb.

Mitch spilled his empty shells to the ground and was reloading as Ben rushed to help Randy up. Ben shoved Randy up by his boot, lifting Randy's belly over the roof's edge enough so he could swing his other leg up and over.

"Thanks," Randy grunted.

"This way," Tucker told them all as well, hurrying across the street toward a ladder. Jake and Baha followed Tucker, leaving Mitch alone outside the door.

"Mitch!" Ben shouted. The first of the moaning townsfolk stepped through the doorway. "Damn it," Ben hissed. Randy leapt up onto the roof and Ben drew his pistol, marching up to the two people at the door and firing a bullet into each of them. They staggered backwards into the other advancing moaning ranks.

"Go on, Mitch!" Ben yelled, stepping backward and firing once more into a third person. Mitch shook the fright off and ran over to where Randy had climbed up, stuffing his pistol into his holster before leaping up onto the post, then jumping to the roof. Ben fired again, looked to where Tucker had led the other three, and content that everyone was safe – for the moment – shoved his pistol into his holster and followed Mitch up to the roof.

The moaning townspeople began fanning out into the street, walking in what appeared to be random directions, noses raised to the sky, sniffing. The two lanterns left on the ground were knocked over and went out, leaving only the waning light of dusk to see by. Up on the hillside where the camp had been Ben could see a line of people coming down toward town.

"What the hell?" Ben asked in shock as he climbed off the awning and up to the rooftop with the others. The woman was sitting, holding her daughter's head close to her, covering her ears and eyes.

"We just called them the dead," the woman told them with a degree of sorrow.

Two

"Thank you, by the way, for saving us," the woman went on.

"Who tied you up in there?" Ben asked, his voice sounding as steady and reassuring as his big frame.

"The survivors," she said resentfully. "They blamed my husband for all of this, so they left me to die when they left town this morning, all heading for Fort Brennan."

"Shoot," Mitch said at that, lifting his hat to run a hand through his blond hair before setting his hat back on. "You didn't happen to see a stranger let out with them, did you? A fat cuss?"

"Mitch," Ben interrupted. "Look, ma'am, we came looking for someone is what my partner here is saying and we were hoping," Ben began and sighed, seeing her eyes so full of remorse and pain. "What's your name?"

"Caroline," she replied softly.

"Well, Caroline, why don't you tell us a little about what it is that's going on here."

"I don't know for certain. I can tell you

what happened.

"My husband Dillon, Dillon Stokes, owned the saloon, the general store over there, and the mineral rights to this hill and about two hundred acres in any direction. He bought it up after the silver mine closed. He was the assayer here before they found the vein, before they mined it all up, and he said there was still twice as much in there. So three months ago he bought it all up and brought us here and hired a gang of Chinese to re-open the mine."

"Ben?" Tucker called out from the other building. "What's going on?"

"We're figuring it out now," Randy yelled back for Ben. He scratched at his silvery beard. "Shut up," he added, pointing toward the heads of the dead down below that were turning and moving toward the noise. The moaning didn't stop. If anything it intensified, and as Caroline continued to tell her tale, the dead below shuffled closer to the buildings, hunting for the source of the sounds they had heard, apparently not knowing it came from above.

"Go on," Ben told Caroline.

"Well, that there was the Chinese camp," Caroline pointed toward the ruined campsite. The line of dead had passed through it and were now at the edge of town. "That's the shaft we started digging. About two months later, they found the first vein. It was small, and Dillon did some measuring and made them go another direction, leaving the silver they'd found. One night he told me his instruments found something else entirely, worth far more than gold or silver. He said it was one of them *new* elements, and that scientists treated the rocks like diamonds they was so valuable."

"Diamonds?!" Mitch said excitedly. "Where are they?"

"Mitch, would you stop interrupting?" Ben asked irritably. Mitch scowled, turning his back on them, his blond hair coming out from under his hat. He lifted his hat and swiped his hair back again.

"Oh, we never found them," Caroline continued. "About three weeks ago we linked the old mine shaft under the saloon with the one the Chinese had been working on. Then the Chinamen all disappeared three nights ago. Two nights ago all the livestock run off, horses, dogs, cats, sheep, you name it. All gone. Some of the townsfolk who live around the other side of the hill went missing too. Then last night all the folks came back, but they weren't right."

Caroline shivered uncontrollably. She looked at her daughter and stroked the girl's hair, smiling to her in the waning light. The girl hugged Caroline, putting her head in her mother's shoulders, hiding her eyes.

"Dillon helped out," Caroline went on. "He figured out first about getting up high like we are. But he died trying to save folks. He got Suzanna and me up to safety, but…never came back.

"This morning there were only a dozen or so folks left. They tied me up in there and took everything of value and started walking the thirty or so miles to Fort Brennan."

"I'm sorry," Ben whispered.

"They tied me up and said I deserved to die for what Dillon had done to them all. They tied up my little girl! How could they do such a thing?"

"They was probably scared," Ben replied. Hateful was more like it, he figured. Hateful that she had come here and brought a horrible plague upon them. "So what do these dead folks do? Why don't they die when we shoot 'em?"

"Lord knows," Caroline said, shaking her head slowly. She let her head fall over her daughter's, gently caressing her hair, kissing her forehead.

"Maybe we're just shooting 'em in the wrong place," Mitch said, spitting over the side of the building onto the heads of the moaning crowd below.

"Would you get back before you fall

over," Ben said.

"I say we try and shoot 'em in the sack," Mitch added with a grin, spitting again.

Ben shook his head in disgust. He, for one, wasn't going to go wasting bullets until he knew what would kill the things. He pulled out his pistol and opened it, digging out the spent rounds and replacing them from his belt.

"I only have about twenty rounds," Ben said.

"Me too," Randy replied.

"We need some rattle snakes," Mitch went on. "Is there someplace rattlers hole up around here? Maybe we can lead them deaders all off there and let the snakes do 'em in."

"Will you sit down?" Randy told Mitch, trying to be a voice of reason. Mitch didn't listen, spitting over the edge of the rooftop once more. His spit missed hitting anyone.

"Damn," Mitch said. "These folks give me the creeps." Mitch backed away and sat down on the rooftop.

"I say we wait them out," Randy offered, scratching at the side of his graying beard. In the dark the silver patches almost seemed white. "It's only nine hours 'till dawn. They weren't out when we rode in. You said it yourself that they don't go about by day, right?" Randy asked Caroline.

"Yup," she replied. "They go back down into the mine shaft come morning. It's like they're afraid of the sun."

"'Cause they're dead," Mitch put in bluntly. "Right?"

"Damn it, Mitch," Randy said sourly, disappointment clear in his tone.

"Hey Tucker!" Ben called out. "We're gonna wait 'em out 'till dawn."

"What?" Tucker called back. "Sit here all night?"

"You got any better ideas?"

Three

So they sat under a slight moon, a quarter of a quarter at best.

"A stampede!" Mitch told them as he took off his boot, letting the grit and sand pour out onto the rooftop. "I bet we could trample all them deaders good that way. That would kill 'em sure enough."

"We don't have no horses," Randy replied. *Thanks to Jake*, Ben thought. "And there ain't no cattle around anyway."

"I'm just saying, it would work," Mitch reasoned. "Or a fire."

"We already talked about that one," Ben put in.

"A cave-in!" Mitch said. "They've got to have some dynamite up in the mine."

"You going to go get it?" Randy asked.

"Well, one thing's for sure," Mitch said sourly, "next one of them deaders I shoot I'm going to put that bullet right down his throat. This moaning is more irritating than a bur in my britches."

They had only been up on the roof about an hour. The deaders, as Mitch called them, had been moaning almost ceaselessly the whole time, shuffling in and out of buildings, knocking things over inside. The things had trouble just getting through doorways, as if they didn't even notice one another. They would push into the other until they managed to trade places. The tiny moon didn't help matters any. Ben couldn't get a good count of how many they were dealing with, but there were at least forty of the things, more than they had bullets that was certain.

"You seen any we shot?" Ben asked. Randy shook his head. Mitch said, "nope." They had talked about it for some time, agreeing that maybe they died slowly from gunshots, like a man does when he's not tended, thinking his wounds aren't mortal. Maybe the things didn't feel pain either. Likely their gunshots would kill them eventually.

"How long does it take to bleed to death?" Mitch wondered aloud. He took his hat off to slide a hand through his blond hair. "I seen a fella live for three days after he got shot in the belly. Damn, if we just had some light down there, at least we could see 'em to know." Mitch slid his hat back on and sighed.

"Ma'am," Ben said softly. "I know it's painful thinking on it, but we need to know if there's anything you remember, something that might help."

"When they eat, they don't pay attention to anything else," Caroline replied. She had told them earlier about how they ate their victims alive, gnawing on the raw flesh like dogs. "Everyone who got bit by one of those things turned into one in a matter of hours. The stable hand got overcome by a pack of the dead Chinamen the first night and the stable master went to help, throwing the things off, trying to save the boy. He got bit for his efforts. Then he turned into the dead and bit five or six others before anyone had sense enough to get away. It spreads like a wildfire and everyone gets to mistrusting one another. I wouldn't even let Dillon near my Suzanna," she said, taking in a deep and painful breath. She began rocking her daughter softly. The girl was sleeping, which Ben thought impossible with the constant moaning.

"Lucky little angel," Ben said, moving a lock of the girl's hair aside. "Must have been exhausted to be able to sleep through all this?"

"Oh, no, she's mostly deaf," Caroline replied.

"Deaf?" Ben asked and Caroline only nodded forlornly. "Lucky indeed," Ben tried a weak smile. Caroline's expression didn't change any.

The moaning was maddening. Being deaf like Suzanna might have been a blessing.

He wondered how it happened to the girl, not really caring so much, but mostly just to think of something, anything, but the noise. His licked his dry lips.

"I bet we could drown 'em if we had some water," Ben put in and Mitch laughed.

"Now you're thinking," Mitch said, standing up. "Let me give it a try!"

"What?" Ben asked.

"I've got to piss," Mitch replied. Ben rolled his eyes while Randy shook his head in disgust. Ben wondered what Tucker and the other boys were talking about. Probably much the same. It didn't really matter which roof he got stuck upon, the men he'd put his lot in with were a sordid bunch. At least Jake would shut up if he was told, though. Mitch, on the other hand.

"Take a good swig of that!" Mitch was laughing from the other side of the roof, pissing over the edge down upon a group of deaders. They moaned dully, ignorant of the slight, looking upward toward the sound of laughter, urine pelting their faces.

"Hey, Ben!" Tucker called out urgently from the rooftop across the street. "I think that one there is Pat Ormsby."

Ben stood up and wiped his hands on his shirt.

"What?" he called back.

"That fat one over there," Tucker went on, but in the dim light Ben could hardly tell exactly what direction Tucker was waving. Ben took a few steps closer to the front of the building and looked around below. It was no use either. He couldn't quite make any of the figures out.

"How can you tell it's him?" Ben called, edging closer still.

"He's the biggest cuss down there," Tucker yelled. "The one that looks like a heifer waddling around just past that group of ten or so in the middle of the road there," he added. Ben couldn't see what Tucker was pointing at. Randy stood near the corner of the roof, by where they had climbed up.

"Do you see him?" Ben asked Randy.

"I don't know," Randy replied. "Wait. Is that him?" Randy pointed.

Ben couldn't see what Randy pointed at from his vantage point. He edged toward Randy, his eyes on the ground below. Suddenly his foot slipped out from beneath him. The sand and dirt Mitch had poured from his boots coated the roof here. Ben fell onto his side, bouncing before he knew it, spinning awkwardly as he pitched over the edge of the roof.

"Ben!" Randy yelled.

His partner's voice sounded so far

away. In the dark he couldn't get his bearings, he didn't know up from down. Ben hit the awning below, his head striking the wood plank. He heard a ringing in his ear. He groped for the edge of the awning and felt it slip away, his body swinging at the end of his extended arm like a pendulum clock, his fingers barely holding long enough to fling him wildly again. His wrist turned sharply and he let go, falling abruptly to the cold dirt, striking face first, hard enough to knock the wind from his lungs. He lay there, stunned, forgetting for a moment the deaders all around him.

Four

Long before Ben fell, Tucker wanted to shoot Jake in the back and throw *him* off the roof. The Mexican wouldn't have cared, and no one would understand him if he tried to explain what happened. More than likely, though, the Mexican would have helped. Ben and the others wouldn't have known what caused it all. What's more, it came with the benefit of a bigger share of the loot for everyone. The Mexican wouldn't complain about that either.

One job! Jake only had to watch the horses, but he let them all get away, and now they were stuck here, watching moaning people shuffle about in the streets below, bumping into one another as though they were blind. They moaned and wailed and walked in and out of open doors, bumping into glass windows like stupid birds, passing by closed doors as if they were no different than the walls around them. *What the hell was wrong with these people?*

One thing was for sure, none of them were right – all of them likely diseased like some rabid dog. Tucker could barely see any of them, but he imagined them frothing at the mouth, dripping blood from the eye, or some other tell-tale sign he'd missed in the saloon. It happened so fast in there. He'd seen Mitch shoot one down and watched it get back up with the same disbelief as everyone else. The only difference was now he questioned Mitch's aim. Had he hit that first one in the chest or in the heart? Maybe these rabid people didn't feel pain, or maybe they were all wearing some kind of steel plates that slowed the bullets. He'd read stories when he was a boy about knights who rode on horseback and wore suits of solid steel. Mitch should have shot one in the head! That would have made sure.

That was the problem with this gang. None of the others were thinkers, except Ben, of course. That Ben Holden was pretty damned smart. He knew how to keep the gang under *his* control. He knew how to plan things out and pull off heists without a hitch. Nothing Tucker couldn't do himself, but with Ben around, well, there couldn't be two leaders, and Ben came first...for now. Losing all their loot to that fat cuss Pat Ormsby meant smart old Ben Holden, leader of the gang, had made a big blunder. Ben needed to fix it, and fast. Tucker aimed to take over if things didn't turn around by morning. All this sitting on the rooftops only made things easier for Tucker.

Which was why shooting Jake right now wasn't the best of ideas. Even though he was spitting mad, Tucker admitted to himself that he needed Jake on his side. Shooting Randy would be better. Get rid of Ben's right-hand man and things would start to crumble, because when it came right down to it, Ben wasn't a killer. He didn't have that kill or be killed instinct a leader of this gang needed. Oh, he'd killed his share of men. He was dangerous sure enough when he took up arms, but he wasn't like the rest of the gang. Reluctant. That was the word for it.

Tucker was a killer.

He should have killed Pat Ormsby four days ago in that bar they'd all holed up in before the heist. That fat son of a bitch called him a coward in front of the gang, all because he'd run off in a gunfight. He hadn't run away. He'd run to get another gun. If Pat had given him his spare, Tucker wouldn't have had to run off, to look like a coward. Tucker never did trust Pat after that, and chasing Pat a hundred miles across the desert proved Tucker right about the son of a bitch.

Take our rubies, will you? We'll see who's the coward when I catch up to you.

"This is dumb," Tucker growled. Sit

here all night, that's all Ben wanted to do? That was his brilliant thinking? What if those moaners down there figured out how to climb? What then?

Tucker glared at the moaning folks in the street below. They all moved slowly, each step rigid like they didn't quite know how to move about.

"Hey, Tuck?" Jake wondered aloud.

"What is it?" Tucker replied irritably.

"Look there. Look at that fat one down there. Don't that look a lot like Pat?"

"What?" Tucker asked excitedly. "Where?"

"Over there," Jake said, pointing across the road under the awning of the saloon. Tucker squinted to see through the shadows. The moon wasn't much, making it hard enough to see anything. With the moaners under the night shadows of the buildings, their shapes could only be made out when they moved, and they moved so damned slowly.

"I don't see nothing," Tucker started to say when a large body leaned one way, turning its head and letting out a wailing moan. "Wait, I see him! That's him for sure."

So he had called over to Ben to get his attention.

What came next took Tucker by surprise. Watching Ben fall off the roof as he did, tumbling in the air and striking the ground hard, stunned him numb. Of course Randy came to Ben's aid, shooting at the nearest moaners and drawing their attention long enough for Ben to come to his senses and stagger to his feet.

"Run," everyone was yelling. Everyone but Tucker and the Mexican. Baha was yelling something in Mexican nobody understood. *That's right*, Tucker thought, *get running Ben Holden or you're gonna get overcome by all those moaners*.

A moaner grabbed Ben by the arm, or maybe just by the jacket – in the dark Tucker couldn't see too clearly. Ben didn't hesitate. He turned to face the thing, leading with his pistol, and fired on the thing square in the chest. The thing staggered back, falling to the ground, and Ben leapt over its body as he moved away from the concentration of moaners all closing in on where it had fallen. Those things were all too dumb to realize Ben was running the other way. They just crowded the fallen moaner like flies on a cow patty.

Tucker's eyes widened at the realization, a wicked smile curling his lips. The stupid moaners were attracted to sound more than sight. Maybe they couldn't see too well in the dark either. Maybe that's why they had such a hard time walking about.

Tucker watched Ben shoulder into a moaner in front of the door to the general store, knocking it off its feet and into the street. He struggled to push open the door against whatever was barricading it inside, slid through the opening, and closed the door behind him before any of the other moaners realized he was gone.

Tucker expected gunfire. He expected seeing the flash of Ben's shots as he fought off some of the moaners who had gotten inside through a back door or something, but nothing like it happened.

"Ben?" Randy called loudly, cupping his mouth to holler louder. "Ben, you alright?"

There was no answer.

"Ben?" Randy yelled again.

That's right, Tucker thought about Randy. Best you start thinking about things in the gang when Ben's gone.

"Quit your hollering," Tucker called to Randy. "I seen where he went. I'll fetch him up."

"What?!" Jake asked incredulously. "You're going down there?"

"If Ben's hurt, he's gonna need someone to help him along," Tucker said. *Help him along in getting killed by one of those moaners*, Tucker thought. "Keep Baha company, and have the ladder ready when I come back."

"How you gonna get down?" Jake asked.

"There's an outside stairway on the next building over," Tucker said, pointing at the building about eight feet away.

"How you gonna get over there?"

"Goddamn, Jake, ain't you never jumped a boxcar before?"

Tucker didn't wait for an answer. He took two steps and leapt across the gap between buildings. His swagger put him in a spot, though. He should have backed up further, taken a longer run at it. He realized that the instant he leapt in the air. He wasn't going to make it. He crouched, throwing one leg as far forward as he could, lifting the other behind him, and hoping he'd just make it. He hit the rooftop square in the thigh of his trailing leg, which dragged him backwards as it scraped against the wood plank of the roof. He rolled and lurched forward, swinging his trailing leg up over the rooftop. He reached out and grabbed at shingles to help pull himself forward, all the while listening to the Mexican laughing behind him, saying something that didn't make any sense.

"I jumped boxcars before," Jake laughed as well, "but none never that wide."

"Shut up," Tucker grunted, hauling his

leg up and rolling onto his back. He lay there catching his breath, looking up at the stars, wondering why he'd done such a damned fool thing as that. *Oh yeah*, he realized, *that bag full of rubies that fat cuss Pat Ormsby had in his satchel.* That's why he was willing to risk his neck.

"Ben!" Randy shouted over the moaning darkness. "Ben, Tuck's coming to get you."

Damned right, Tucker thought.

Five

Ben put his shoulder to the stack of boxes to slide the barricade back into place against the door. The scraping of the boxes over the wood floor was too loud, he thought, but leaving it unprotected didn't seem smart either. He turned to face the darkness of the store, his back against the barricade, expecting to find a hundred deaders just waiting for him. The darkness inside the store gave no hint of movement. Large shapes up to his waist, barrels or stacks of crates Ben guessed, took up space on the floor sporadically. A long counter filled the right side of the store. In the back, a square of light from outside broke the otherwise utter darkness within. He could see the gray expanse of the hillside through the open door.

"Shoot," Ben breathed under his breath.

He tried to draw his pistol again and winced at the pain. In his flight from the deaders outside he hadn't realized how badly he had been hurt. He'd felt some pain for sure, but his adrenaline and fear drove him like a frothing horse, pushing him past the point of pain or resistance to action that was catching up with him now. He held the side of his arm, rubbing it gently to test whether he'd broken it or not. It seemed fine, but tender and sluggish.

Ben cautiously shuffled through the debris on the floor, side stepping his advance, gun leading the way. He slid his front foot forward to be sure nothing was there to trip him or make noise, then he shifted and brought his back foot up next to it. Every few times he paused and held his breath to listen.

He heard Randy calling his name. That was all he could make out. Even the moaning of the deaders was quieter inside the store. All the windows out front were still intact, so he glanced back from time to time to see the swaying of a form shambling along the elevated side walk in its meandering quest for whatever it was drawn too. So far the only thing for sure that the deaders went after was live people, but Ben suspected the livestock and animals hadn't all run off. Some, like the animals in the stable or chickens in a coup, probably got overcome by deaders and eaten.

Ben shivered at the thought of a pack of deaders bringing down a full grown horse or cow.

Ben leaned his head out the hole where the back door should have been. He looked both ways, taking a deep breath of relief when he didn't see any deaders. The door, however, was lying flat on the ground, having been torn off its hinges. With another wince of pain, he holstered his pistol and stepped around the door. Bending low brought another pain to his left leg, a searing and sudden pain from his hip that rose to his spine. His grunt escaped through clenched teeth despite his will. His heart began to race. He hoped none of the deaders heard him. With his good arm he lifted the door and stood with the strength of his good leg. He didn't have the strength to fit the door in place properly, nor the time. To his right he heard a moan that sounded as though it was just around the corner in the alley.

Ben propped up the door into the frame at an angle, leaving a space just wide enough to slip through for himself. He had to draw in several quick breaths to slow his heart as he continued backing into the store, away from the mostly covered doorway. He hoped that would be enough to keep the deaders from seeing or hearing him.

Don't make a sound, he told himself, coming to a stop in the middle of the store. He looked behind him through the glass windows at the main street. Three deaders shuffled close enough for him to see them. They were all three going toward the stable area as though they meant to leave town. For a second he hoped they all might just do that. Maybe he'd have a chance to get back up on the roof that way.

He didn't hear it so much as sense it. He drew his pistol, wincing again at the pain in his shoulder. He aimed toward the back door before his head turned to look. He could see the shape of something slow moving past the gray triangle of moonlight outside, he could hear its moan louder than all those in the street out front. In the distance he could hear Randy calling out again, saying something unrecognizably muffled through the closed doors and windows of the store. He watched the shape outside the back door, its slow meandering search taking it closer to the rickety door.

I can just shoot it and run, Ben thought, but then remembered he had used up a few shots already. He wasn't sure how many bullets he had left.

The back door creaked as the deader pushed against it. Ben sucked in his breath, raising his pistol a little higher. The moaning from beyond grew frustrated. The door shook, banging in the recesses of the door jamb. For a moment Ben thought it would fall through for sure.

His heart jolted again at the sound of

wood scraping. He turned toward the front of the store quickly, his pistol leading the way. He saw the widening gap of the front door and heard the distant and urgent calls from Randy. *What was he saying?*

Again the door rattled behind him and he looked back to make sure it still held. The door lifted away from its socket in the jamb, straightening toward the sky. The deader was figuring it out.

The scraping from the front stopped and Ben heard labored grunting as though someone were pushing through the door. Ben pulled back the hammer of his pistol with his thumb, raising the barrel toward the front door. A body pushed through and fell to the ground.

Ben began to squeeze the trigger.

"Don't shoot," Tucker gasped and Ben took his weight off the trigger, sighing. "Ben, don't shoot me."

Tucker drew in his legs and pushed the door shut with his feet. Ben didn't say anything. His heart pounded loud enough. He turned his attention and his gun toward the back door. The door banged against the jamb, startling Ben enough that he shuddered.

"Ben? You in here?" Tucker asked, the scraping returning as he pushed the barricade into place against the front door. A thumping came at the front door as though fists were striking it.

"Hush!" Ben hissed. The scraping stopped, but the thumping against the front door continued. So did the rattling against the back door.

Tucker took two steps away from the front door and collided with one of the barrels, toppling it, knocking something heavy that was on top of it to the ground loudly.

"Shoot," Tucker growled even as the noise of something metal scraped as it swayed side to side, taking what seemed like an eternity to come to rest.

"Quiet!" Ben snapped, speaking through gritted teeth. "There ain't no back door."

Tucker started side stepping, drawing his pistol and aiming toward the back.

"What's that then?" he whispered, waving his pistol toward the door. In the nearly pitch black it did no good. Even Tucker couldn't see his own gun. The door shook in answer, arching backwards into the darkness like a drawbridge, toppling over and falling to the ground. The door fell on top of the deader, swaying wildly as the inhuman being struggled to free itself from underneath.

"Shoot," Tucker said in response. "There's stairs across the way. We can maybe jump to the roof."

"Come on," Ben said, leading the way. He tried his best to hide his limp. At the doorway he glanced both ways. There was a group of three deaders coming from their right and two more to the left. The one under the door was nearly halfway out.

Tucker stepped past Ben and put his pistol to the deader's head, pulling the trigger. *Blam*! The thing jerked at the impact and began flailing wildly.

"Damn it!" Ben snapped.

"This way," Tucker said and started leading them straight out, away from the buildings and toward the desert. Ben didn't say anything at first. He didn't want to draw any attention their way. Instead, he followed Tucker to the edge of the flat dirt, to where the sage brush reached into the border of the town. Ben turned around to see if any of the deaders were following.

The group of three were swaying toward them, fanning out with rigid strides as though they needed to plant each foot before trying the next. The other two that had come around back were curled over the deader Tucker had shot.

"Well that solves that," Tucker said, stepping up beside Ben. "How many rounds you got?"

"Only a few. I need to reload."

"Then reload," Tucker said, stepping boldly toward the oncoming trio of deaders.

"Tuck," Ben tried to argue, but Tucker already had his pistol raised squarely in the face of the nearest one. He fired, the blast ringing so loudly Ben thought the whole world could hear. The one he shot stumbled to its knees, its head falling listlessly toward the grayness of the bare dirt, leading its body into a heap. It began to shake and contort as Tucker aimed his revolver at the thing's head once more, firing with a loud *Blam!*

"Would you stop shooting?" Ben demanded. "You're going to draw every last one of them."

Tucker backed away from the remaining two, expecting them to fall on the body between them. One of the deaders stumbled into the body and halted, unsure, moaning its discontent. The second deader kept marching toward Tucker like a wind-up soldier, snapping side to side with each stiff step.

Tucker fired again. *Blam!* The nearest deader lurched backwards like being hit with a bat, but didn't fall.

"Damn," Tucker spat. "Missed his forehead." Then he fired again, the impact knocking the deader backwards. It fell square on its back and began shaking on the ground.

The third deader, having abandoned the first body, fell onto this second one, biting at it around the head and neck where blood and gore spilled out the two wounds Tucker's shots had produced.

Tucker grimaced at the sight, standing only a few feet away, pistol pointing at the third moaner, ready to take its life too.

"Tuck," Ben warned. Tucker looked up and saw more shuffling figures coming around the buildings on all sides.

"You reloaded yet?" Tucker asked.

"I haven't even started," Ben replied.

Tucker spat, firing his last round into the head of the third moaner hunched over the body at his feet. He stepped back as the thing shook violently over the body of its partner. Tucker spilled his spent bullet shells to the ground while stepping up next to Ben.

"It's days like this I wish I wore two guns," Tucker said with a grin. Ben could see the whites of his teeth and eyes even in the gray light of the slivered moon. The moaning moving toward them came like a roar. Ben opened his pistol and shook the bullets into his hand to fish out the good ones. He'd need all the ammunition he could spare for a fight like this.

Six

Gorges squinted into the darkness. They called him Baha, sometimes The Baha Kid, because that's where they thought he came from, but Gorges didn't mind. He liked the name. It sounded like the name an outlaw would take. It sounded menacing and tough. The thing that irritated him about this gang, though, was that only Randy and Pat ever understood some of what he said, and even they could only spit out a few words in Spanish, enough to get by. Ever since Pat ran off with the rubies from the heist, Gorges wondered if maybe it was time to find another gang. Pat couldn't be trusted anymore, and he didn't like Ben very much. About the only one in the bunch he'd throw his hat in with now would be Tucker.

After the first shot, Gorges wondered if maybe that was the end of Tucker. Then more shots echoed through the night, and as Gorges looked toward the hills, peering into the darkness in the hopes of spotting movement or the glow of guns firing, he began to wonder if maybe this was as good a time as any to get out. How far could the horses have run off, after all? They were tired before ever getting here. If he could set out on foot the way the beasts had run off, he might be able to catch up to them by morning. If not, at the very least he'd be getting away from this town. The devil was at work here.

He shook his necklace for protection, kissing one of the dried ears.

"What do you think's going on?" Jake asked. Gorges couldn't understand him. He scowled at the young gringo. He'd let the horses escape. No one would care if he just pushed Jake off the roof right now. No one would know what happened. *Why bother*, he thought at last, sighing with disgust.

Instead he slid the ladder down to the emptying street.

"What are you doing? Where are you going?" Jake asked. Gorges understood the concern in his tone but could only make out "go." He knew that word. He pointed toward the other end of town.

"Al diablo con diablo," Gorges grated. "Estoy dejando." With his rifle in one hand he swung a leg out onto the ladder and began climbing down.

"Wait," Jake said. "Hey Randy!" he shouted. "Randy, the Mexican's climbing down too!"

"What?" Randy called back.

"The Mexican. He's climbing down."

"¿A dónde vas?" Randy shouted, but Gorges didn't reply. Once on the ground he jogged up the street toward the stables, making his way around a few devils ambling in the street. They didn't move very fast, these devils, which was why he was surprised by a dark figure that turned toward him from the shadows of an awning near the general store, so much so that he fired his rifle into its chest from fright.

The devil fell to the ground. Gorges looked around. None of the other devils were close enough to be of concern yet. He made a vicious whack with the butt of his rifle across the moaning devil's eyes, cracking the thing's skull. It convulsed from the impact and Gorges, the Mexican, the one they called Baha, knelt down with drawn knife to retrieve another ear for his collection.

Jake hesitated, unsure whether to pull the ladder up and wait where it was safe – alone – or climb down after the stupid Mexican to see where he was going. What did he mean, diablo diablo? That was the devil, wasn't it? Had he seen the devil?

"Shoot," Jake finally spat, working up his courage. At the very least, he could cross over to the others on top of the saloon if the

Mexican got into too much trouble.

The echo of gunfire was near and far now. Jake saw Mitch standing atop the saloon, shooting down at a crowd of moaners in the alley. Off behind the saloon and general store Jake heard a few shots snapping in the distance where Tucker or Ben must have gone. Then the echo of the Mexican's rifle filled the street and everything stopped, even Jake. He could see a shadow slump to the ground ahead, then the tell-tale shape of the Mexican, his wide sombrero turning this way then that, as he crouched down next to his latest victim. Goddamn sickening thing. Just like the Indians and their scalping rituals.

Jake jogged over to Baha and put an arm on his shoulder.

"Come on," Jake urged. The moaners around them were coming closer.

Baha spun, pointing a bloody knife up at Jake, saying "no me toques!"

Jake withdrew his hand and raised both in surrender, stepping back.

"Alright, alright, Baha. Just get it over with and come on."

Baha laughed while turning his attention back to the moaner's head. He slid the knife behind the second ear and began carving. The moaner's head shuddered and lurched, turning toward the pain, leading with its teeth.

It wasn't as dead as Baha had thought.

"¡Ay, caramba!" Baha shrieked, beating the moaner's head with his other fist. The moaner hissed, letting go of Baha's hand, frothing blood dripping into its open mouth as it turned its teeth toward the punches. Baha lifted the knife and plunged it into the thing's eye socket. It began shuddering from head to toe. Baha jumped back, one hand holding his wrist.

"What the hell?!" Jake asked, stepping beside the Mexican. "Come on," he added, slapping Baha on the arm. "Get your gun."

Baha mumbled an oath and a prayer as he reached down to pick up his rifle, his eyes hardly straying from the corpse laying on the street.

"Come on!" Jake insisted. Baha took two steps back from the body and bumped into Jake. Only then did he look up to see how many of the devils had managed to shuffle closer. They were surrounded by at least a dozen, leaving no direction they could run without shooting their way through.

"You stupid ass," Jake said, drawing his pistol.

Seven

Mitch squinted into the darkness toward the hillside. He'd seen the last shot just before hearing it, an orange spark like the zap of a lightning bug. Randy was yelling out to Ben, cupping his mouth and shouting Ben's name with the concern of a dog locked out of the house. Randy was Ben's right hand man, after all, so seeing Tucker, instead of Randy, climb down into the street to go save Ben was a real shock. When the first shot rang out Mitch figured one of them was shooting the other, but then Randy pointed out two men running away from the buildings.

"You think they're running off?" Mitch asked, spitting over the edge of the roof down onto the deaders, all packed together like cattle for slaughter. He nodded toward the hillside when Randy looked at him. In the dark Randy couldn't see, but he knew who Mitch meant.

"Where would they go?" Randy asked.

Mitch shrugged.

Before he could answer, though, Jake shouted something about the Mexican. Randy shouted back, crossing the roof to the front part facing the street between them. Mitch listened, but kept an eye on the deaders down below, splitting his attention with glances toward the hills, wondering what Ben and Tucker were doing.

Mitch watched the deaders turn toward the front, following Randy's shouting. What stupid idiots, he thought of them all. Just following the nearest noise. What the lady said about them, though – that they would feed on you alive – that gave Mitch the creeps.

If only he knew where that fat cuss Pat Ormsby had gone. Mitch would shoot him dead – at least deader than he already was. There was no way that the fella he'd shot in the saloon was still down there shuffling around in the dusty street. That one had to have died by now. It was just a matter of shooting them in the right place, or waiting for them to bleed to death. Like chasing a stag you only hit in the flank. He'd die soon enough.

Mitch wanted Pat Ormsby to waddle out like a fat sow. He'd empty his pistol into the son of a bitch for getting them all into this mess in the first place.

"Quit your shouting," Mitch grumbled toward Randy, who was trying to speak Mexican into the darkness. "You're attracting…"

His words stunned himself. He hardly

heard the snap of another round being fired off along the hillside. The realization of what he'd thought up, that he'd discovered something all on his own, caused him to grin up one side of his face.

"Ormsby," Mitch sang into the darkness, drawing his pistol. "Oh, Ormsby, you fat cuss. Come out, come out where ever you are!"

Then he fired down onto the crowding deaders below him. He may or may not have hit one. It didn't matter to him. He just wanted to make some noise. More noise than the others. Enough noise to draw all the deaders back. Pat Ormsby would stand out in a crowd. Mitch smiled and fired his pistol again.

"What the hell are you shooting at?" Randy snapped, coming over beside Mitch to look down.

"Well, I had me an idea," Mitch started explaining.

"Stop wasting your ammunition, for God's sake."

"Then what do you want me to do, curse at them?"

"Don't do nothing! We gotta figure how we're gonna get to Ben!"

"Ben!?" Mitch shook his head. "I ain't going out there," he said, waving his gun toward the hills. Another snap of a pistol firing echoed in the darkness, a blink of light off a ways too far to see clearly who fired or what was happening. "Besides, it sounds like they're doing fine on their own."

Mitch pointed down and fired again. One of the deaders stumbled.

"Yes!" Mitch hissed triumphantly. "Got one."

"Would you please stop shooting?" Caroline said hotly. Mitch and Randy turned to regard her. She was cupping her daughter's ears, cradling the girl in her lap.

"Why? She can't hear nothing," Mitch replied and fired down into the alley one more time, not even looking at his target. Two more guns started firing from up the street, a pistol that went off three times and a rifle that fired twice.

"What the?" Randy asked, side stepping toward the front of the building.

Mitch swore and fired two more times into the deaders down below. That son of a bitch Jake and the filthy Mexican were out there riling up the deaders.

"Stop shooting!" Caroline yelled. "You're scaring her."

"I thought you said she was deaf!" Mitch replied.

"Only mostly," Caroline explained. "She hears loud noises like guns. You're scaring her."

"You sure it ain't the deaders doing the scaring?" Mitch mumbled, pointing down with his pistol and firing his last round.

"Mitch, quit it!" Randy shouted.

"I'm out of bullets now anyway," Mitch said. He opened his gun and poured the empty shells over the ledge onto the deaders. The shells sprinkled down into the darkness. "Eat those, you sons of bitches," Mitch said and spat again. "Hey, if you ain't gonna use your bullets, how about you hand me some?"

"Mitch, stop wasting 'em," Randy replied.

"Fine," Mitch said, pulling new bullets from the back of his belt and reloading. "When I get me those rubies, though, I'll keep that in mind and take the difference out of your share."

"What are you talking about?" Randy asked, perking up.

"Don't you want to hear my idea?" Mitch replied with a grin.

Eight

Ben stepped in front of Tucker and fired, shooting another deader square in the face. He had only shot two so far. Tucker, on the other hand, had emptied his pistol twice and was reloading as quickly as he could. The deaders, now having Ben and Tucker in sight somehow, kept coming like a mudslide. As one toppled over, stumbling to the ground in a shuddering heap, another took its place. Sometimes the deaders would descend on their killed companions with a ravenous lethargy, as though taking more pleasure from the slow plunge than the actual gnawing and rending of the flesh. With teeth alone they bore down on the body, biting out chunks from the arms and neck. They avoided the heads and faces mostly, preferring places in which they could sink their teeth on meaty, raw flesh. They used their hands simply to prop themselves up over the body, using their own torsos to hide their meal from others like the wings of a vulture.

"This is stupid," Ben said, fighting back his revulsion at the sight of another deader collapsing over the one he'd shot, slowly plunging, teeth first into the neck. Further back, deaders were rising from the bodies of the ones they had shot previously. The flesh of the already dead didn't seem to satisfy. They wanted Ben and Tucker. "We're going to run out of bullets before we run out of them deaders. They just keep coming. I think they're attracted to the noise."

"What did you call them?" Tucker asked.

"What?!"

"What'd you call them? Dead 'ems?"

"Dead 'ems?" Ben said queer. "Tucker, what the hell are you going on about?"

"You called 'em something."

"Who cares what they're called?!" Ben snapped, lifting his pistol and shooting another advancing deader. It stumbled backwards but didn't fall. Ben missed in the dark. There was a trick to where to shoot them. Off to the side a little too much and it only blinded them or broke a jaw. It didn't kill them the same way a shot straight into the nose would. Or a shot from the side right above the ear.

Another gun blast came from the rooftop in town. Ben could see it light up in the distance just before the sound of it struck. Something was going on there too, and he worried Randy was doing something foolish like trying to find him. Ben hadn't heard

Randy's voice in a while.

"Well, we'd been calling them moaners on account of all that moaning they do," Tucker said.

"The woman said they were the dead, so we've been calling them deaders," Ben explained, backing away from the lumbering figures in the dark.

"I like moaners better," Tucker replied, closing up his pistol. "How many bullets you got left?"

"I dunno," Ben said, feeling around his belt to get a rough estimate of about eighteen more shots. "A whole lot less than there're moaners or deaders or whatever you want to call them."

"I bet there're bullets aplenty back at the general store," Tucker said, walking sideways, following the outskirts of town. Ben kept up with him, but so did the deaders. Maybe they could smell them, Ben thought. Maybe his and Tuckers' voices were enough to draw their attention. Maybe they could see just fine in the dark.

"If we lead them to that campsite, I bet we can run and double-back around them," Ben suggested. "Maybe get back on a roof until sunrise."

"Why? With bullets we can kill them all."

"That's just stupid," Ben replied. "If we kill them all, and the army arrives in the morning, what do you think they'll think? That a town turned into deaders and we had to fight for our lives, or that a pack of gunslingers killed everyone over a sack full of rubies?"

"What makes you think the army's coming?"

"Well, if you'd got up on *my* roof with that woman, you'd know the surviving townsfolk headed out this morning for Fort Brennan. Them army boys will probably ride out here just as soon as the sun rises."

"Then all the more reason to get them rubies and get the hell out of here, don't you think?" Tucker asked. He stopped walking. The deaders were shuffling toward him in the sage brush, winding around it like fresh rain runoff coming down a hill.

"Keep walking," Ben said.

"I'll run when I'm out of bullets," Tucker replied. He faced the oncoming horde, what looked like at least fifteen to twenty deaders. There were still more getting back up after their feeding.

"Fine," Ben said, looking up the hillside at the encampment. "Hold 'em off and I'll take a look at the camp site for anything we can use."

Tucker shot the nearest deader, waiting

until it was only a few feet from the end of his pistol. Its head snapped back and it convulsed and fell backwards over a large mound of sage brush. The other deaders paid it no heed. Their moans grew louder, almost mocking Tucker's resistance. *Sooner or later*, it sounded like the deaders were telling them.

Too bad none of the deaders had gun belts, Ben thought. They were regular folks of all ages, mostly Chinamen in this bunch. Tucker had shot two of the children and a woman. Thankfully Ben had only faced two grown men so far, and even with them he couldn't quite get over the notion that these were still people they were slaughtering. If only they would just wake up from whatever spell they were under. If only it was as easy as splashing water on their faces, or just waiting until they wore off their drunkenness. Anything was better than killing them in cold blood.

The Chinamen's camp site had been fairly well destroyed and reeked of death. It looked trampled, as though a struggle had taken it down, and those who survived simply abandoned it – if anyone had, indeed, survived. Ben lifted the first canvas tent flap to find a half-eaten body. He jumped back from the sight, expecting it to rise up and start moaning like all the other deaders. After that, he figured the mounds inside the tents weren't going to be supplies after all, and he sure as hell didn't want to go in there looking regardless. Instead he kicked around the crates and toppled barrels looking for boxes the right size to hold bullets, a weapon, a lantern, or anything useful. What he found was mostly tools for working in the mine, jars of food stock, sacks and pouches of all sorts, hair brushes, clothes, and every other kind of useless supplies for a time like this.

Three more rounds echoed from Tucker as four rounds went off in town.

What the hell was going on up on the roof tops, Ben thought, squinting to see through the grayness of the night. He could make out the buildings – he even convinced himself he saw Randy and Mitch up on one of the rooftops and Jake and the Mexican on another.

"Find anything?" Tucker asked as he climbed up the slope to the camp.

"Nope."

"Which way you want to run for it, then? I'm running low on ammunition."

"How about we run on down around that way toward the stables and see if Jake got any of our saddle bags off the horses before he let them run off?" Ben replied.

"Sure. The store's right across from it."

With that, Tucker began to jog off

along the hillside, leading the way. At first Ben thought Tucker was running funny because they were moving along the hillside on uneven ground, but when they started straight down the hill, he could see Tucker's gait clear enough.

"Why you limping?" Ben asked, struggling himself to keep up. He slowed and put a hand on his own back. Running down the hill was sending spikes of pain up his spine. He straightened and groaned.

"I got hurt trying to jump between buildings in the goddamn dark," Tucker said irritably.

"Hey, I can't run so fast," Ben admitted. Tucker slowed too and looked back, giving Ben a chance to keep up. "That fall knocked me around something awful. I ain't feeling too dandy."

"Well, we're a good distance ahead," Tucker said with a wave. Ben looked back to see the horde they had collected marching in a wide line down the hillside. "We can stay ahead of them."

"Agreed," Ben said, walking past Tucker. "Just don't stop for nothing."

Nine

Goddamn Mexican, Jake thought. He should be shooting Baha in the back instead of these moaners. None of them were dying anyway, he reasoned. The only problem with shooting the Mexican was that it likely wouldn't kill him, and he'd shoot back. The moaners, even the one wearing a holster, didn't have any guns. Good thing too because if any of them were smart enough to use one, even the rooftops wouldn't have been safe.

Jake fired his third shot into the moaner blocking their way. The Mexican cranked his rifle and fired over Jake's shoulder at the same one.

"Jesus Christ!" Jake yelled, startled by the gun blast. His ear rang and he turned around to glare at Baha. "Watch where you're pointing that thing."

"¡Vámonos!" the Mexican said, motioning ahead with the tip of his rifle, cranking it again. Jake looked ahead at the hole left by the collapsed body of the moaner. He didn't need an interpreter to know it was time to run for it.

The other moaners were closing in on them, close enough now that there was no way between them without at least one of them being able to reach out and grab them. That's what worried Jake more than anything, that one of those moaners would grab hold of him. They'd latch on like a leech and hold him until the others could amble over, and then they'd all consume him, pull him down to the ground and suffocate him under their weight, just like the two ahead were doing to the twitching body of the moaner Jake and Baha had filled with bullet holes. The two moaners sprawled themselves out over the twitching third, their two heads butting like Billy goats, their teeth reaching for the soft flesh under the chin. Jake put a hand over his own neck and flung himself past, through the opening they'd left in the wall of remaining moaners.

"Come on," Jake said, pointing toward the building they'd abandoned. Even in the darkness he could see the ladder still there. The Mexican ran past him, straight for the stables. "Where the hell you going?" Jake demanded. He looked back at the ladder and saw a figure moving beneath it. *Damn it all*, he thought, chasing the Mexican instead. If nothing else, the Mexican would stumble into any moaners first.

The interior of the stables was nearly

pitch black by comparison to the grayness of the outside. Even the meager light of the moon hardly penetrated, except through the open door of the hay loft overhead. The Mexican started climbing a ladder nailed to the wall that led up to the loft.

"Where you going?" Jake hissed, looking out the wide open stable doors, thinking he should close them up to keep the moaners out. There was a groan from the darkness behind him, somewhere in one of the stalls. "Shoot," Jake said, holstering his pistol. "Climb faster!" Jake rushed to the ladder.

The groans grew louder as several other unseen moaners started struggling to find their way to Jake and the Mexican. The Mexican swore each time he tried to hoist himself up with his right hand, flinching at the pain where he had been bit. He held his rifle with his left so he had no choice but to keep climbing with the pain.

"Move it, move it," Jake demanded, lifting himself up as high as he could, putting his hands between the Mexican's legs. In the dim light Jake could make out one of the moaners creeping toward him like a shadow stretching with the setting sun.

"¡Ay!" the Mexican gasped from the pain, almost losing his grip. He reached his arm through the ladder, hooking it rather than using his hand. His hand felt like he had burned it in fire. It felt like a scorpion sting. It reminded him of his youth, long ago days wagering for a few pesos and a bottle of tequila by betting to see who was man enough to take the most stings. This pain was worse.

"Get your fat ass up the ladder!" Jake yelled hysterically.

"Sal de mi culo," Baha growled, hoisting himself up one more rung.

It was too late. The shadow had eyes that floated like moths in the firelight, arms that felt like the reach of darkness, hands that grasped Jake by the ankle. It was amazing how strong the moaner was. It felt like the thing put all of its weight to the task of trying to wrench Jake off the ladder. Jake slipped a rung and reflexively hooked his right arm into the ladder. The swiftness of the moaner's jerking dragged Jake along the wooden cross members that acted as steps. As Jake screamed and reached up desperately to hang on, he felt his thigh press against the wood and catch on something. It was his holster that saved him, but in that split second it spilled the one thing he needed, his gun. The pistol poured out of the holster, the strap that usually tied it to his leg snapping under the force, allowing it to tip upside down.

"Shoot, shoot, shoot," Jake repeated

fiercely. "Baha, Baha!"

Jake tried kicking the moaner, but it did no good. The thing must have felt no pain, and when Jake took his other foot off the rail, the moaner's weight just started dragging him down.

Baha looked down at the scene without pity. The son of a bitch was getting what he deserved. Leaving the horses the way he did, letting them get away. Baha looked up and braced himself to reach for the next handhold. He swept his hand around and hooked the ladder with his elbow, lifting his whole body.

"Baha, you son of a bitch!" Jake screamed, lunging upward, lifting the whole weight of the moaner with him. The moaner clung to Jake's leg, hauling its head ever closer. Apparently it figured if Jake wouldn't come down, it could pull itself up to feed.

Jake grasped Baha's rifle and wrenched it from the big Mexican's hand. The weight of the moaner was too much for Jake. He slipped down a rung. He wanted to figure a way to use both hands to turn the rifle face down, but as he grabbed the barrel of the rifle with his right hand, he felt a new sensation on his foot.

He screamed in pain as the moaner sank its teeth into his toes.

"God damned son of a…" he started to shout angrily, pounding on the moaner's face with the butt of the rifle. He slammed it into the thing's skull like a butter churn - *wham, wham, wham!* With each strike he clearly heard the cracking of bone, three, four, five times before the thing let go.

Without the rifle, Baha climbed several rungs higher using his good hand. He wanted to shoot Jake for stealing his rifle, but his shooting hand felt like fire and twice as big as it should. He could barely move his fingers, which meant he couldn't draw his pistol to kill the son of a bitch.

"Shoot," Jake exclaimed as he shook the pummeled moaner off his foot. He lifted himself up out of the thing's reach and gingerly put his foot into the ladder to support himself. The moaner sank into the shadows of three or four other figures jockeying for position below.

"Damn it, Baha, get your ass to the top!"

Ten

"That's the dumbest idea I've ever heard," Randy said.

"What do you mean?" Mitch snapped.

"It ain't gonna work," Randy replied. "Besides, we'll run out of bullets before you spot Ormsby."

"What do you know?" Mitch groused.

"He's right," Caroline told him. "There should be near a hundred and fifty people all told down there. How many bullets have you got left?"

"A fair amount, lady," Mitch snapped. "Look see, I got us two or three dozen of them deaders down below already. Any minute that fat cuss is gonna show. Any minute."

"Fine," Randy sighed. "Give me the matches. I'll go get it."

"Now you're talking. I know it'll work! You'll see."

"Just stop wasting all your ammunition. They're coming, like you said. Make your racket some other way."

"How?" Mitch asked.

As way of answer they all heard Jake

scream from the stables.

"Shoot!" Mitch swore.

"What in the?" Randy asked.

They knew the yelling and screaming was Jake's, but they couldn't make out what he was saying. Whatever he was yelling, it sounded urgent, and desperate.

"You think he's getting eaten?" Mitch asked hopefully. Randy just looked square at him. "What?" Mitch shrugged. He shook his head, looking down to avoid Randy's glare. His eyes grew wide as he pointed toward the ground, saying, "hey, shoot!"

The deaders at the edge of the group Mitch had corralled were turning toward the stables, toward the screaming.

"Hey! No you don't," Mitch yelled. "Don't you go running off!"

"Gimme the matches," Randy said, slapping Mitch in the chest with the back of his hand. He didn't like Mitch's idea, but hearing Jake's scream unnerved him enough that doing anything was better than waiting around, waiting for that to happen to him too. He'd already lost Ben to the darkness, and now it sounded like Jake was a goner too. He hoped Ben was still out there. The last gunshots they'd heard from up on the hill came from near that abandoned mining camp. Randy hoped Ben hadn't been dumb enough to go down there.

Mitch fished the box of matches from his vest pocket. "Bring back a bottle of anything you can find."

Randy snatched the matches as Mitch began yelling loudly and stomping his feet on the roof. He yelled curses and tried to sing a song of which he hardly knew the lyrics.

"Be careful," Caroline told Randy as he stepped beside her. "It's not just sound that draws them in. Any light and they flock to it like moths."

"Good to know," Randy told her. He paused, noticing in the darkness the concern in her voice. "Just don't talk to him and you'll be all right," he added, nodding toward Mitch, who was still shouting and making a ruckus. "The more you mix with him, the more he goes on."

"Good to know," she said, smiling weakly.

"I'll be right back," Randy said. He took a cautious step to the eaves and put a foot out on the awning of the second story windows. The first window was open and he stepped through quietly, expecting a deader to be lurking in the shadows. Inside was nearly pitch black. He wanted to strike a match, to see where he was going, but thought better of it. *Stick to the plan*, he told himself, even though it was a dumb plan. Mitch always came up with dumb plans.

"So who's dumber, him for thinking it, or you for doing?" Randy asked himself, shuffling his feet across the floor with a hand out in front of him to feel for a wall or anything that might be in the way. He edged a foot forward, sweeping it slightly to make room for his footing and advanced toe to heel, toe to heel across the room.

He bumped into the dresser, hissing a curse to himself. With his hands he followed it to the wall which led him to the open doorway and out to the interior balcony. He didn't dare leave the wall along the balcony in the darkness. He didn't know if the railing would hold him, or where exactly it was, but he did know that a long drop stood between him and the floor. With his hand leading the way, he side stepped to the first flight of stairs.

Each step felt as though the world ended. As he put his foot down, he expected to find nothing there, yet each time was surprised when he struck purchase. The wood beneath him creaked, but the noise of it seemed less than the thumping and muted shouting coming from Mitch up on the roof. At least there were no deaders in here. They would have been groaning and shuffling his way for sure.

A gray sliver of moonlight cut the floor

in half from where it came in at the front doorway. A window beside the doorway cut a second, wider line, enough that Randy could see how to get outside from the edge of the collapsed stairwell. The sound of the deaders moaning outside came muffled and dull. Nothing inside stirred as he stood at the last landing. He took a deep breath and held it, reaching a leg down along the wall where the last flight of stairs had been hacked off, sliding the tip of his boot down to where he hoped the chair was still propped against the wall. His toe reached it so he put his weight on it and stepped down into the darkness, landing hard, not knowing where the ground would be. He stood up straight and listened, his eyes panning across the room. Still the only sound was the muffled groaning outside and the dull thumping of Mitch's boots on the rooftop.

Randy let out his breath.

As he made his way toward the front door, each step taken gingerly, his boot testing the ground before he put his weight ahead, he wondered if the deader Mitch had shot earlier was still in here. It was so dark he couldn't tell if the uneven looking ground was from shadows cast by fallen or broken chairs and tables, or a deader laying in a heap. He felt a shiver run up his spine at the notion.

At the front door he looked out into

what appeared to be a deserted street. He stood still, tilting his head one way, then the other. The awning above him cast a line of black shadow across his chest. The rest of the world was a muted gray of thick outlines that seemed to all be moving as his eyes darted this way and that. He trusted his ears instead. The moaning was coming mostly from around the corner, in the alley where Mitch had managed to wrangle up the bulk of the deaders.

Randy walked out into the street, trying not to make any noise over the wooden side walk. Once in the dirt of the road, he trotted over to where he had last seen their lantern. It appeared as nothing more than a large stone, its shadow making it wider than it really was. The glass reflected the sliver of moonlight as he approached it.

"I see you, Randy Miller!" Mitch yelled from atop the roof. Randy felt flush with anger. He wanted to tell Mitch to shut the hell up. He turned to look up at the roof instead, drawing his hand high in the air to show his finger.

"Randy's got balls as big as a bull! You hear that deaders? Don't rile him or you'll get the horn."

Mitch kept yelling out nonsense at the deaders in the alley, stomping his feet and singing words that didn't fit his tune. Randy scooped up the lantern. As he started moving, though, the sound of a deader to his left gripped his heart. He nearly leapt into a full run, but managed to calm down, reminding himself that the things weren't as fast as that. He looked toward the groaning of the deader and could see a large form teetering one way, then another, in slow, unsteady motions.

Randy hurried into the saloon anyway. Once inside his step took on more caution again as he felt his way forward, trying to avoid making any noise that would attract the deader outside. He didn't head for the stairs, though. As much as he thought Mitch's plan wouldn't work, he had to agree that having a length of rope long enough to reach the ground might come in handy. The only problem was, in the dark he couldn't tell the long ends from the short where Ben had cut out that woman and little girl.

Randy knelt down at the post to feel around the rope with his hands, searching for ends to unravel. As he worked he looked over his shoulder and listened for any noise coming in through the door. Any minute he expected that deader to shamble in and start lumbering its way toward him. When he wasn't looking over his shoulder, he peered around the post toward the bar, thinking that maybe more of the deaders might come up from underground.

And all the while, becoming more annoying with every passing minute, was the sound of Mitch's boots thumping on the roof. Randy began hating Mitch's calls echoing around him, the groans of several dozen deaders in the alley, and even the creaking of the walls as they pressed their bodies against it. Randy wondered at the scratching sound coming through the walls, imagining it was the deader's fingernails as they tried to climb to get to Mitch.

Randy looked behind him again, certain there was something in the doorway.

Nothing.

He found the end of the rope and started to unravel it from around the post. They had tied the lady up good. What a horrible thing it was, too. If not for Ben and them all coming when they did, she and her little girl would have been…Randy shuddered again, taking a deep, steadying breath. He spun around once more, dropping the rope and reaching for his revolver. He plucked it out and pointed it toward the door and window, watching, waiting. Still nothing moved. Still all he heard was the thumping of Mitch's boots above, the dull and endless moaning from the alley. It was maddening.

Then the shadow appeared. Randy's heart throbbed, his body went rigid, and he sucked in a desperate, quick breath. The lump in his throat felt like he'd swallowed a fist. It was a deader for sure. It came around the door as though it had found its way from the alley. Randy must have seen its shadow when it passed by the window earlier, but only recognized it after it had passed, when the dim light of the moon came in again.

Randy wanted to run for it, to stand up and run back to the stairs, to get away, but the fear deep in his gut weighed like an anchor, holding him down. He remained huddled, ready to leap up and strike, but otherwise as motionless and silent as he could be in his little spot in the shadows.

The deader didn't groan like the others. It took rigid, clumsy steps, lurching forward slowly. Randy only began to breathe when he realized the thing wasn't walking toward him, but instead into the center of the room. The time it took for Randy to regain his senses was about as long as it took the deader to reach the center of the room. Only then did Randy berate himself for letting the thing cut him off from escape back up onto the stairs. He looked toward the doorway, expecting another one of the things to be there, blocking his only other means of escape.

Well, not the only one. There was that door in the floor behind the bar, the one leading down into whatever hell the deaders came up out of.

The deader kept moving, shuffling its feet through the debris, uncaring of the noise it made or the clutter it disrupted. It moved to the back of the room and around the bar, and then it found the hole and began to make its way into the depths of utter darkness beyond. As its head dipped out of sight, Randy stood to watch, to make sure that was, indeed, where the thing was going.

Then it was gone.

Jesus! Randy thought. It hadn't even seen him. Randy wondered only a moment about why it had gone back down the hole, more grateful that the thing was gone than anything else. He knelt down again and felt around for the rope, but with his hands shaking and his nerves on edge like they were, he couldn't be sure which end he had been holding in the mess of it.

He wiped the sweat from his brow, realizing he couldn't do it without light. Mitch had been right when he said "you're gonna need matches to see what you're doing."

Randy's hands were shaking as he slid open the box of matches. *Don't drop any*, he told himself, trying to get control of his fingers. *Plenty of time once you light it. Those things move slow as molasses.*

His thoughts didn't reassure him, though. Maybe they moved slowly in the dark because they couldn't see too well. Maybe with the light they would move like normal people and all rush in here on him. Maybe the one that went down into the hole would come running out.

Randy struck the match. It hissed, nearly blinding him. His fingers trembled as he slid open the hood of the lantern and touched the match to the wick. It lit up easily and Randy shook the match out, sliding the hood back in place. Randy turned to face the door and window, his own shadow rising up the length of the wall.

Shoot, that's bright, Randy thought. Like a lighthouse beacon he'd seen back in California years ago. It could probably be seen for miles.

The length of rope he'd been working lay on the ground. He scooped up the end and started measuring arm's lengths. He knew what he had was too short just by looking at it. His head turned in every direction as he counted, four, five, six. He listened to the moaning outside change. Even the pounding of the boots moving as Mitch tried to keep the deaders' interest. Randy could hear Mitch yelling louder, stomping his way across the rooftop, nine, ten, eleven. He spun the loops of rope he'd made around the post three times to loosen more, then struggled to slip it through a knot. Just another two or three lengths is all he needed.

The moaning grew louder and he heard the first thump against the glass of the window outside. He shifted his position to crouch behind the beam so he could watch the deaders while trying to untie the knot. The deaders put their hands on the glass and pushed it, their faces thumping on the thin pane where the inverted words Stokes Saloon arced like a rainbow. Randy was able to loosen the knot enough to slip the whole wad of rope through, but his heart was pounding and the sound of the deaders grew with the tempo of insistence of Mitch's pounding of his feet on the rooftop.

A shot rang out and Randy stiffened. It came from the roof, he realized. Mitch was doing everything to keep the deaders outside, but it wasn't working. Randy could see a shadow forming in the doorway, then another.

"Goddammit," Randy growled, tugging the rope around the post one more time. "Good enough."

Randy yanked his knife out and started sawing where the rope knotted up again. The moaning inside the saloon was as loud now as it had been outside when he was on the roof. Randy looked up to see four shapes now, one getting entirely too close.

The knife slipped through, cutting the rope free. Randy dropped the knife and yanked out his pistol. He took two steps forward and raised the gun to the nearest deader's head.

"Sorry," he said and fired.

The deader's head snapped back, blood splattering out the back of its skull and onto the other deaders. The body of the one he'd shot began twitching as it collapsed to the floor. Randy didn't wait to see what happened next. He turned, grabbed the lantern by the handle, and he ran across the room.

The deader he'd shot shuddered and the next two behind it, still covered in blood and gore, swooped over the body like vultures. Their groaning turned from haunting moans to vicious snarls. At the collapsed stairwell landing, Randy lifted the lantern, rope, and his gun up and dropped them so he could get a hand hold. He put a foot on the chair and jumped, his hands flat on the landing to help pull him up.

He fell back.

"Son of a…" he snapped, then tried again.

The moaning sounded so loud it may have been right on top of him. He grunted, trying to haul himself up, looking back at a line of deaders only a few feet away. He swung his legs, trying to swing up higher, but it was no use. He couldn't get his leg over the top. How the hell had that little woman done it so easily? He swung a leg up and missed.

"Shoot!" he cursed.

A shot rang out just over his head, startling him. He almost fell back, but had sense enough to hold on.

"Come on, you fat ass," Mitch said, kneeling down and grabbing Randy by the shoulder of his jacket. Mitch fired his pistol over Randy's head again and Randy looked back to see a deader fall. They were so close now their arms reached out and almost grabbed his leg as he hauled himself up.

Mitch dragged him away. Randy scrambled for his pistol and turned around with it to shoot the nearest deader in the face. The deader's heads were at the level of the landing and for the first time, thanks to the light of the lantern, Randy could see they weren't human. They were dead – the living dead.

A man's skin tone changes after death, that much Randy knew. He'd seen the purpling that looked like bruising on the down-side of a body before. A face down man would go purple in the face, but a face up body went purple on the ass end. It didn't matter what way they were facing after about a day, though. The head and neck turned greenish-blue and the skin sagged so much it looked like an oversized shirt on a too small person. The only difference between the deaders and a real dead man were the eyes. They weren't sunken and dried out, bleeding or dripping puss like he'd seen. On the deaders, their eyes were fierce and desperate, like a wild dog starved all winter long.

"Come on, get up!" Mitch insisted. Mitch picked up the lantern and rope as Randy backed away and got to his feet. They both ran up the steps and to the doorway to the roof. As soon as they were both in the room, Mitch closed the door to hide the light. He held up the lantern to have a look at Randy. For a second Randy thought maybe Mitch was concerned he was hurt. He looked at himself as well, holding his arms up to look inside of his jacket.

"Where's the whiskey?" Mitch asked.

Eleven

"What in the blue blazes?" Ben asked, coming to a stop. He could see the light on the saloon rooftop. Tucker held up next to him, looking both ahead and behind, gauging the distance of the moaners following them.

"Come on, they're catching up," Tucker said and started limping ahead.

"How are they catching up?" Ben asked, looking back. "Damn," he added, seeing that the nearest deaders were only twenty feet back now.

"Them two are fast," Tucker said. "We probably should just shoot them now."

Ben winced as he took another step. His hip had gotten worse coming down the hill and with every step he felt a searing pain shoot into his lower back.

"Maybe they're excited about that light," Ben said. "Where did Randy get that lantern?"

"Who says it was Randy?" Tucker asked, his annoyance plain to see. Ben didn't answer. He hobbled past Tucker to get ahead on the trail again. The street through town had several tall shadows swaying, slowly moving toward the light. Some figures were coming out of the doors of the buildings across the street from the saloon. Ben could only faintly make them out, but he could tell the difference between the gray shadows that moved and the normal shadows that looked like buildings and a broken wagon.

"Let's get inside the store and barricade it again. We'll be able to fend them off from there."

"What are we gonna do about the back door?"

"One of us will have to watch it while the other looks for bullets and guns."

"Fine," Tucker said. "You watch the doors, I'll find the bullets."

They both hobbled and dragged their wounded legs into town.

"Look at all the deaders," Ben pointed out, stopping again. He took a deep, calming breath in the hopes that it would cut down on the pain. "They *are* attracted to the light."

"That's Mitch," Tucker said, stopping beside Ben. They could both make out the taller, skinny frame of Mitch. Randy stood behind him, a rounder shape in the orange glow. "Come on," Tucker added, slapping Ben on the back. "They're gaining fast, gimpy."

"I don't want to climb up on another

roof," Ben sighed.

"Me neither," Tucker agreed. It was the first thing they could agree on all night. With enough bullets they wouldn't need to.

"Hey!" a voice called. It was Jake. Tucker and Ben kept walking, but looked toward the left side of town where they'd heard him calling.

"Jake?" Ben called back.

"Would you shut it?" Tucker hissed at Ben. "You want to announce to all them moaners we're here?"

"Ben!? Is that you? Hey, this goddamn Mexican tried to run off. We're up here in the hay loft. The sick bastard cut off a moaner's ear and he's up here trying to add it to his necklace.

"Hey, is that Tuck with you? You two look like a couple of moaners. I was thinking of shooting you until you both stopped and looked around."

"Shut your hole!" Mitch called out from the rooftop of the saloon.

"We're going for more bullets," Tucker called to Jake. "Cover our backs!"

"I thought you said to be quiet," Ben ribbed.

"What was that?" Mitch yelled. "Is that Tucker with you now?"

Jake started yelling, trying to explain

what he could, as Ben and Tucker hobbled to the empty sidewalk in front of the store.

"After you," Ben whispered. He didn't want to put his back into pushing the door open again. Tucker sighed, but pushed it open anyway. Ben watched the street as the two deaders who had been following them made their way toward the stables, toward the nearest loud noise, which was still Jake yelling to Mitch to tell him how he almost shot Ben and Tucker thinking they were a couple moaners.

Ben and Tucker slipped into the darkness of the general store through the opening Tucker had forced. Outside Mitch and Jake argued about what to call the things, deaders or moaners. *What the hell did it matter*, Ben thought? Ben stood dead still, waiting, holding his breath and expecting a deader to shuffle toward them in the dark or reach out from a shadow. He knew Tucker was by his side, holding his breath the same as Ben. Tucker took in a deep breath and sighed it out. Nothing moved. The only noise reaching them was that constant dull, muffled moaning echoing every direction and the muted conversation being shouted between the two rooftops outside.

"Close it up," Ben whispered, taking a cautious step toward the back door. "I'll go guard the back."

Twelve

After watching Ben and Tucker hobble into town, Jake thought maybe the two of them had gotten into a fist fight or tussle, or maybe shot one another in the leg. They looked a lot like moaners, which made Jake wonder if maybe they were turning into moaners. After all, they were coming down from the mine shaft. What if there was some kind of snake or animal up there that caused all this, or what if that camp site had some ghost or witch doctor, or more moaners?

"Hey, Baha, should I have shot them?" Jake asked.

"No entiendo," the Mexican replied. Jake looked back at the shadow of the Mexican and shook his head. It was no use. He couldn't understand a word the Mexican said. Baha sat cross legged with the moaner's ear he had cut off in front of him. He swung his normal necklace of dried ears in circles above it, mumbling words in his gritty language.

"You sure you ain't Indian?" Jake asked.

The Mexican said nothing.

"Give me some more bullets," Jake said. The Mexican looked up questioningly. "Bullets!" Jake said again, pointing at the repeater, then toward Baha's belt across his chest. "Give me your damned bullets so I can reload."

"Gilipollas," Baha growled, but lifted the belt over his head and tossed it forward. At least the stupid gringo would help him reload.

"Yeah, yeah, gilopagos! Whatever you call them. Bullets!"

Baha sneered. *Push him off the loft. Leave him to the devil. That's what Gorges should do to that pain in the ass.*

The pain in his hand had eased, but now Gorges' fingers and arm were numb. The scorpion-like sting he endured had reached his shoulder earlier, then shot throughout the rest of his body, spreading like boiling water poured over his skin. In the dark he had clutched his necklace of ears and whispered a prayer for protection, which seemed to have worked. The searing pain settled after a minute, leaving him weak and tired, but now the numbness was growing up his arm at an alarming rate.

The devil takes me, Gorges thought. El Diablo had come for retribution, to take his soul and spirit from his body, in a manner that felt as though he were ripping it out of Gorges still living flesh. The pastor from his youth was right after all. Gorges tried to remember the words he was supposed to use to beg God for His forgiveness, but he could barely think straight. The darkness in front of him grew wider, the sounds around him louder.

"Oh, Dios," Gorges groaned, hunching over as pain drove into his stomach.

Jake knew that word – adiós. It meant goodbye. "Where do you think you're going again?" Jake asked hotly, turning the rifle toward Gorges. The Mexican swayed forward and backwards over his pile of ears. A disgusting ceremony, Jake thought. Saying goodbye to the departed like that was just wrong. Of course, collecting their ears in the first place was the behavior of a savage anyway. Jake turned his attention back out the loft door. He didn't want to even witness something so godless.

"You're disgusting, Baha," Jake grumbled.

Gorges' hands trembled as he held them out, groping for the sound. What was it? He swatted at the air, raking his fingers through emptiness. El Diablo? Why had it become so dark? Was He here, or had He already come and collected his soul to bring it to hell? He lurched forward again, the crippling pain in his belly causing him to slump forward onto his hands. He was helpless in its grip, able only to let out a low moan in pain. He looked up to see a sparkle of light in the distance, an orange glow around which a sound shook him from head to toe. In his prostrate position he knew what it was. The glow of the fires of Hades and the voice of El Diablo coming to take him. He dropped his head as the pain coursed through every fiber of his body.

"Oh, for the love of Pete, would you shut the hell up?" Jake snapped. "It's bad enough hearing all them moaners."

Jake looked over the ledge of the open hayloft door at a moaner making its way into the moonlight, attracted to the lantern light atop the saloon just as the rest of the long line of them coming down from the hillside. Jake wondered how Mitch and Randy had got a lantern to see by. It sure would have made it easier loading the rifle. Jake slid another bullet into the loading gate alongside the receiver of the rifle, then looked out of the hayloft window again. He lay on his belly and took aim with the rifle. Why not shoot one, he thought? All that carrying on the Mexican was doing was irritating him.

He took aim at the back of the fat moaner just below, watching it sway in jerking fashion, imagining it was Baha in a drunken stupor, shaking his necklace of ears and singing in that foul sounding language of his. That fat cuss Pat Ormsby and Baha spent a lot of time talking in it too.

"Jesus, Mary, and Joseph!" Jake exclaimed getting up to his knees. "Hey, Baha, look here!" Jake could hardly believe his eyes, but he knew that brown satchel anywhere to be his own. That son of a bitch moaner down there was Pat Ormsby, and that satchel hanging across his shoulder and behind his back was full with their rubies. "Hey, Tucker!" Jake shouted. "Hey, Ben!"

A hand closed onto his leg like a vice, yanking him by the ankle and pulling him hard and fast. Jake fell forward, trying desperately not to fall through the open door of the hayloft. He landed flat on his belly and felt himself being dragged backwards, back toward the ladder. For an instant he had an image of that moaner that grabbed him earlier at the top of the ladder, its hand stretched impossibly far, eyes as wide as its hungry mouth, hauling him back for a second bite. Jake rolled to his back as he slid, trying to figure out what was going on, saying "let go!"

It wasn't the moaner. Baha was on his hands and knees, one hand outstretched and pulling Jake closer, a starved moan pouring from his bearded maw.

"Get the hell off me!"

Jake kicked Baha's hand with his other foot, but that did nothing. The Mexican finished dragging Jake close enough to lift his foot toward his mouth. Jake planted his other boot onto Baha's forehead and tried to pry himself free. Baha's head rolled back under the force, but the big Mexican's grip didn't slacken.

"Let go," Jake said fiercely, pointing the rifle at Baha. The Mexican sat up abruptly, dragging Jake again, and before he knew it, the Mexican had grabbed his other leg too. Jake couldn't see the Mexican's face to shoot him there, and with his feet so close he didn't even want to try. He swung the repeating rifle between his legs and fired.

Baha snapped backward, pulling Jake with him. Jake shook his legs but Baha still held him as fiercely as before. Jake cranked the rifle and fired again. One foot slipped out of the Mexican's hands and Jake kicked at the Mexican's face, cranking the rifle one more time. Jake aimed a little higher than before and fired again, somewhere around the shoulder because Baha spun sideways, throwing Jake's leg and spinning him as well. The blast knocked the Mexican backward enough that where he landed was the edge of the loft, and with that momentum, Baha pitched over and fell into the darkness.

Jake lay on his side, wide-eyed, gasping, disbelief hanging in the air along with the scent of dry straw, gun smoke, and cold sweat.

"Baha!" he blurted, crawling forward to look down. He'd shot the Mexican. He'd actually shot one of the gang. "Baha," Jake called down into the darkness. "Get up and run!"

His plea was met with groaning as a shadow rose from a heap on the floor, the unmistakable wide brim of the Mexican's hat turning upward to look at him.

"Dear God," Jake breathed, thinking of how Ben and Tucker had started looking like moaners, and now Baha had gone crazy too. "You're one of them!"

Thirteen

"Have you ever even ridden as a cowhand?" Randy asked irritably.

"What do you mean?" Mitch snapped. He didn't like the implication of Randy's words.

"That's the worst excuse for a knot I've ever laid my eyes on. Give me that rope."

"No, it's my idea, my knot. Besides, this ain't supposed to be for cattle. We need a *hangman's* noose."

"Well then you're still doing it all wrong," Randy said.

Mitch was about to argue the point when he heard Jake calling out for Ben and Tucker. Both Randy and he looked toward the stables. Even the woman sitting on the roof with them looked up in wonder. She was as worthless as a mute, Mitch figured, not worth a damn, her or her deaf daughter. A sudden snap of gunfire from the stables startled him, a tiny jolt of surprise tightening every muscle.

"What in the?" Randy thought aloud. Another shot went off, cutting off his words.

"Here, you do the tying," Mitch said,

pushing the rope into Randy's hands. He stepped toward the corner of the roof that looked out over the stables. Another shot rang out. "That's Baha's repeater. You think he's killing Jake?"

"¿Qué está pasando?" Randy yelled. Mitch figured Randy thought the same thing by the way he used the Mexican's language. He laughed to himself. It served Jake right for losing their horses. Sooner or later someone was going to put a bullet in him.

"Stop talking Mexican!" Jake shouted back. He sounded pissed off, almost hysterical.

"What the hell's going on over there?" Mitch shouted.

Jake didn't answer right away, making Randy and Mitch look at one another, wondering.

"He tried to kill me," Jake yelled back, his voice under control again. "I shot him."

"The Mexican?" Randy called back.

"Yeah, the Mexican! Who else do you think was up here with me?"

"Is he dead?"

"I dunno. He fell off the loft." The only sound to be heard for a moment was the moaning of the deaders in the alley below. "He tried to kill me, I swear!"

No one said anything. Randy took a step closer to the woman, his head downcast as he looked at her. Probably trying to comfort her or make her feel all right about it, Mitch thought. Mitch just sighed, thinking that the better of the two was dead. He sort of liked the Mexican, even though he didn't understand a damned word he spoke.

"You still got his repeater?" Randy called out.

"Yeah."

"How many bullets?"

"At least fifty."

"Fifty?" Mitch hissed, surprised. "How'd he get fifty bullets for that thing? He'd need that belt Baha always wears--"

"I know, I know," Randy said quietly. "He ain't telling us everything."

"He can hit us with that repeater from there," Mitch added.

"I said I know," Randy snapped. "Let me think."

"Hey, fellas?" Jake called. "I just seen Pat Ormsby coming your way."

"Well why didn't you shoot *him*?" Mitch yelled out.

"I was about to when Baha…" Jake's voice trailed off. "Right before he tried to kill me. Hey, are Ben and Tucker up with you?"

"We ain't seen 'em," Randy called back.

"Hey, Randy, look," Mitch said

excitedly. "There he is! There's that son of a bitch Ormsby coming our way."

"You see him?" Jake called out.

"Yeah, we see him," Randy yelled back.

"He's still got the satchel," Jake added.

Mitch mumbled, "you mean *your* satchel."

"Shut up about that," Randy said. "Pat tied him up and stole it."

"Sure, that's what Jake said."

"He was tied up when you found him!" Randy reminded Mitch emphatically. "You saw it with your own two eyes. Do you think he tied himself up?"

"No, I just think it was too easy for Pat to get his gun from him and tie him up and take the rubies, is all."

"Oh, and what would you have done if Pat put a gun to your back and yanked your pistol out of your holster when you weren't looking?"

"I wouldn't have been dumb enough to let Pat get behind me."

"Pat always brought up the rear, and you never had anything to say about it before."

"Sure I did. I called him a fat, lazy, son of a bitch plenty."

"Ever to his face?"

"Hey, Pat!" Mitch hollered into the

darkness with his hands cupping his mouth. "Yeah, you, you fat, lazy, son of a bitch! I'm gonna get you." He turned to Randy with raised eyebrows. "There," he said.

Randy rubbed his eyes. He was getting tired, and not just of Mitch. The night had been dragging on for some time, and after a long day's ride in the hot sun all he really wanted to do was sit down and wait for morning. Age did that to a man. Made him slower on the draw, heavier in the saddle, and harder on the eye. At least going down into the saloon and out on the street had pumped new energy into him for a while, but the feeling wore off by the time he reached the roof again, leaving him weak in the knees, exhausted, thirsty, and hungry too.

Mitch took out his pistol and waved it toward the darkness. "Do you think we should shoot Ormsby a few times before we catch him?"

"How the heck are we supposed to get a noose around his neck if he's flat on the ground?"

"I dunno. I'm just thinking is all. He's here," Mitch said, pointing his pistol down at the big shadow they knew to be Pat Ormsby. Even as a deader he limped from that old bullet wound in his left leg. Being shot by the law was the reason he turned from a law abiding rancher to a robber like the rest of them. The fat son of a bitch joined Ben's gang about a year ago, before they picked up Tucker in a saloon brawl. If they had found Tucker first, Ben probably never would have agreed to let Pat join, but now they were stuck with him. That was Ben Holden – a man of misunderstood morals. They kept Pat even though they didn't need him for much because, as Ben put it, Pat hadn't asked to leave and he hadn't caused any ruckus, which probably led to why Pat broke from them after their last heist. He knew he wasn't wanted, so why not break away clean and rich? The size of their haul was too much for Pat to resist.

Who among them wouldn't have done the same given half the chance? Ben had been smart to put the least likely two in charge of the loot. Pat was old and slow – at least they'd thought so – and Jake was young and stupid, or at least Randy thought so. With the Mexican killed, Randy wasn't so sure about Jake anymore. He wasn't sure of anything since sundown.

"You gonna lasso him or not?" Mitch asked.

"Huh?" Randy said, realizing he still held the rope. "Oh." He started feeding out the noose enough to give it a try. Mitch's knot sagged, the loop of the noose almost straight, but he didn't want to pull it up and re-tie it.

Mitch would only argue the point and try it himself a hundred times before he'd let Randy fix it. One failed try and Mitch wouldn't be so objectionable.

Randy played out the noose as he swung it below.

"Why don't you get the lantern to help see?" Randy complained. Mitch slung his pistol and moved over to get the lantern. As he held it up, Randy let the noose fall. It came down close to Pat, landing on the head of a deader in front of him. Randy congratulated himself for getting so close. He reached out to pull up the rope.

"You missed," Mitch said idly, holding the lantern high over the edge.

The deader the noose landed on reached up and grabbed the rope as it rose from its shoulder, yanking at it, turning viciously as it hunched down while biting into the knot. Randy, rope clutched tightly in his hands, pitched forward, gasping "Jesus", only letting go of the rope too late. He groped at the air in front of him, swinging his hands furiously as though he might be able to fly enough to steady himself, to hold his balance. He felt his hand hit something. Maybe it was Mitch reaching out to save him. Randy turned and reached for him, but doing so spun him precariously sideways. He looked back at Mitch's wide eyes in the orange glow of the lantern as he slipped off the roof.

The fall felt endless. Mitch held a hand out toward him, but the distance between them compounded and in the time it took to suck in his breath and tense for impact below, the lantern light retreated like a bullet, shrinking to the size of the very stars themselves. He struck the ground like being kicked by a horse, turning and toppling over something, then again rolling in midair before landing on his knees. His momentum spun him toward the ground on his side, but he didn't quite make it. He felt his shoulder strike something that gave way with him, and he realized he had fallen into the horde of deaders, toppling several in the process.

"Oh, dear God," Randy groaned, reaching for his pistol. He rolled onto his back and looked toward the sky. It was studded in shimmering white rhinestones. Several shadows lurched side to side, blotting out parts of the sky, closing in over him. He pointed at the nearest and fired. He shot again, pushing with his feet to slide backwards, but he was completely ringed by deaders. The one over his head began to lean over him and he shot that one twice, then the one to his side. He shot and shot and even though he ran out of bullet he tried to shoot again. He could hear the snap every few times he pulled the trigger. Perhaps God was reloading for him, but through it all he realized the blasts came from above.

"No!" Randy screamed as another deader fell onto him, its whole body trapping him under its weight. Randy put his hands out to stop the heavier, bigger figure, that of Pat Ormsby – *Jesus Christ if he weren't a heavy son of a bitch* – but the weight of the fat cuss and so many other bodies that came tumbling over him crushed the wind from his lungs. His scream faded as he felt the first painful bite sink into his shoulder.

Mitch held the lantern high and shot the last of his bullets into the deaders. With Randy's shooting, the rapid snaps and the bursting cloud of orange sparks everywhere, the air lay heavy with the smell of sulfur. Randy's scream cut out suddenly. Caroline clutched her daughter's ears, her body blocking the sight of Mitch standing alone over the writhing mass below. It looked to Mitch like a bucket full of maggots down in the alley. Mitch stepped back and looked over his shoulder at the woman and the girl, thinking that he couldn't have had any worse luck.

"What's going on?" Jake yelled from across the street.

Mitch slumped down to sit and reload in the lamp light, avoiding looking over the edge or toward the stables. Jake called out again and Mitch held his tongue rather than yelling something nasty. That little son of a bitch still had that repeater, and in the lamp light Mitch was an easy target. He poured out his empty shells into his hand and threw them over the edge into the darkness.

Mitch blew out the lantern and sighed. He didn't want to see anything right now. He hoped the dying light would lure the sight of what he'd seen back out of his eyes so he could somehow forget, but his hands shook in terror. It could have been him, was all he thought. He took out his pouch of tobacco and paper. He needed a cigarette. What he wanted was whiskey, but he'd settle for a cigarette. Mitch pat his vest pockets and sighed.

"Shoot," Mitch said to himself. "He didn't give me back my matches."

Fourteen

Ben and Tucker heard the gunfire. The snap and pop came so loudly through the wall it startled them both. Tucker dropped all the boxes of matches he'd found, crouching quickly while drawing his pistol. Ben pushed his back against the wall and looked both front and back, head turning between them with every shot, trying to decide which way the noise was coming. It came from behind him mostly, at ground level, in the alley. *What was going on*, Ben wondered?

Tucker felt around on the floor for the matches, picking up a couple of boxes as he listened. He remembered seeing all the moaners down in the alley. That meant one of the others had gone in there and started shooting them all up.

"You don't suppose they came looking for us, do you?" Tucker whispered as the gunfire played out. It sounded like a dozen shots in all. They'd gone off so quickly he hadn't thought to keep count in his head.

"That would be dumb," Ben whispered. "You found any bullets yet?"

"No, but I got some matches. If I light one--"

"Don't go drawing attention *our* way!" Ben whispered harshly. His back still ached from all the walking after his earlier fall. Running from a pack of deaders and trying to reload at the same time, in the dark, was the last thing he wanted.

Tucker had other ideas. *We could make a stand if we had light and enough bullets*, he thought, *if Ben and the others weren't such cowards*. He'd show Pat Ormsby who was afraid of a fight. Light up the place to draw him in, and then *blam*! He'd show that fat son of a bitch.

"Are you looking?" Ben whispered. Tucker shook his head to rid himself of old thoughts. He was still crouched low with pistol in hand. He huffed and shoved his pistol into its holster to keep up the search. The moaning outside still echoed from the open back door, filling the room enough to mask the soft noise of his foot sliding across the junk strewn floor, or when his hands gently felt around the contents of the shelves, pushing and sliding things, knocking them over from time to time.

He was most worried about spiders. Getting bit by one in the dark to be more precise. Some big, fat black widow so old and mean the store owner probably gave it a name and left it alone, never selling that can of beans or box of nails it anchored its sticky, thick nest to. He imagined the spider gliding down on an invisible line to land on the back of his hand, sensing his warmth. Its tiny fangs would dig into one of his veins in the hopes of making a gusher of blood from which to drink.

The only thing worse would be snakes. A mean rattler sleeping out the night, not licking the air so it wouldn't know Tucker was there. He'd reach a hand out and touch its firm, smooth back, coiled up like a rope, and out of instinct it would strike. Only after sinking its teeth into Tucker would it start rattling its tail.

He reached a hand to his belt where he kept his knife to make sure it was still there. An X incision was how you sucked out the poison of a snake bite. He'd have to be quick. He wondered if it worked on spider bites too.

"Hey, Ben, why don't we switch places a while," Tucker said, wiping a hand over the beads of sweat forming on his brow. Goddamned spiders and snakes and this blinding dark getting him so worked up. He'd rather go fight the moaners than chance getting bit in here.

"Just don't light any matches," Ben said, edging toward him. Tucker waited by the wall behind the counter so he could show Ben how far he had gotten in his search. Ben reached Tucker and held out his hand, whispering, "give me the matches."

"You don't trust me?"

Ben didn't answer the question. Of course he didn't trust Tucker. "If I find the bullets, I'll need to read them to know what size."

"Just grab them all!"

"I still want the matches," Ben insisted.

"They're on the floor," Tucker replied, stepping past him. "Get as many as you like. See if you can't find a lantern while you're at it."

Ben winced as he knelt down. The pain in his back was getting worse. He wondered how badly he'd hurt come morning, then berated himself for thinking like that. Morning was hours off. He had to survive the night first. He needed to get those rubies off of Pat Ormsby before the cavalry rode in. Of them all, only Pat, Tucker, and the Mexican were wanted men. The law didn't know the names or appearances of Ben and Randy, nor Jake. Mitch was the son of a mayor in Texas, so if anything happened to him, he'd be let off Scott free. The real trick was to just not be here in the morning, and thanks to Jake, that meant more walking. For once, he agreed with everyone else. He wanted to shoot the little pecker.

Ben slid his hands across the floor and felt the small boxes of matches. He grabbed a box and stuffed it into his vest pocket, then started looking for more. His hand brushed against an uneven board. He slid his hand sidelong and felt it dip and start again, still uneven, as though he had reached the joint between two boards. He slid his hand back and followed the uneven split the other direction to find it suddenly turned ninety degrees. With both hands he followed the outline and realized it was a rectangular cut-out in the floor.

"Hey, Tuck," Ben whispered. "Did you feel the floor over here?"

"Yeah, it's a little uneven," Tucker replied from his perch at the edge of the hall leading to the back door.

Ben continued to feel for anyplace there might be a handle. His hand passed over the last edge of the rectangle and he felt cool air rising against his fingers.

"I think there's a trap door here," Ben said.

"What?"

"In the floor. I think I found a trap door leading down."

Ben swept his hand across the floor, feeling several of the boxes of matches. He scooped up three and put them into pockets as quickly as he could, not letting his other hand leave the joint of the door in the floor.

"Let me see," Tucker said as he moved softly across the floor.

"What are you doing?"

"I want to see."

"Guard the door," Ben insisted.

"That one you found *is* a door, so I'm gonna guard all three."

"Just shut up."

"How big is it?"

"I said," Ben began and caught himself. His voice had raised. "It's big enough," Ben replied at a whisper, calming himself as he felt around for anyplace to dig his fingers under the boards. "Look, that woman we found said her husband owned the mine and that he had a tunnel running from the saloon all the way up to the top. If this goes to that tunnel, we can get over to the saloon without bumping into any of them deaders and we can come up under and get on the roof with Mitch and Randy."

"So what," Tucker said. "If you find the bullets I can go out there and gun down every damned moaner that gets in our way!"

"Would you pipe down," Ben replied softly.

"Let's get some more bullets before trying the hole or going outside or anything," Tucker whispered.

"Fine," Ben agreed. He stood slowly,

the ache in his back driving up his spine and down his right leg. "I'll keep looking for bullets."

Fifteen

Mitch sniffed, clearing his nose, then spat over the side. He slid his pistol into his holster after reloading it, then stood, looking back at the woman.

"I suppose you'll be wanting comforting or something," Mitch grumbled.

She didn't answer. In the dark he could barely make out her eyes. He knew they were glaring at him, though. He could feel it.

"You got any matches?" he asked her, tapping the lantern with his foot.

"No," she said.

"Any water or food?"

"They tied me up to die," she told him, as if his line of questioning were absurd.

Can't blame them for trying, Mitch thought as he looked down over the alley at the mob of deaders. Those that had fought their way onto Randy's body early had been pushed out of the writhing ring, even Pat Ormsby. The fat son of a bitch tugged on something long and slender, pulling it in a vicious tug of war with another deader. The two snarled and growled and carried on like bobcats over a hawk wing.

Pat Ormsby won, ripping the piece of long flesh from the other deader's grip, turning abruptly to shield his prize with his back.

Jesus, Mitch thought, realizing what he had witnessed. *That's an arm*!

Sure enough, Pat Ormsby lurched out of the pack toward the street, guarding a bloodied stump of an arm, gnawing on it where the bicep once met the shoulder.

"Jesus," Mitch said aloud, unable to contain his shock and revulsion. Even as much of an ass as Randy sometimes was, he didn't deserve to get torn up and eaten alive like that. Up until now, Mitch hadn't really given much thought to the situation they were in. These deaders were an inconvenience and only about as dangerous as any mob of people. But normal people didn't do that. Normal people fell down and stayed down when you shot them. Normal people ran from gunfire. Normal people would have been afraid of Mitch and the others. And normal people certainly didn't eat you alive.

"Jesus," he breathed again. He edged along the rooftop, following Pat Ormsby as he left the alley and headed for the saloon. He watched the fat deader amble under the awning, wondering aloud, "where the hell you going now, Pat?"

"Back underground," the woman answered.

Mitch spun around and turned his ear toward her, stepping back up beside where she sat. "Huh?" he asked, head tilted in confusion.

"The ones that feed go back down into the mines, back to the gas chamber."

"How do you know all this?"

"Because my husband figured it out. He went down there with a few of the men to put a stop to it. Only a couple of them made it back. The ones that eat go down there to rest in the gas chamber."

"Gas chamber?"

"The place where the stuff leaks out. It's like a pool of gas the way my husband described it. None of them went into it except for Dillon. They were all too afraid. That's how my husband got bit by one of the deaders. He couldn't see it under the surface."

Mitch shook his head. She was just trying to scare him, he reasoned. He backed away from her and made his way for the window back into the saloon. It didn't matter what kind of ghost story she was trying to scare him with, Pat Ormsby was getting away.

"You'll need a lantern down there," the woman said.

"I ain't got any matches," Mitch snarled as he ducked into the room. He used his hands to find his way to the far wall, then edged to the door and out onto the interior balcony. He looked toward the front door but there was no movement.

"Pat!" Mitch sang mockingly. "It's just you and me now. Where'd you go?"

As way of answer, a bottle fell to the ground at the bar beneath where he stood. Mitch moved as quickly as he could to the other end of the balcony to get a better view. He could only barely make out a wide shadow as it descended behind the bar counter.

"Oh, no, no, no, no," Mitch said. "Pat, don't you go going down there!" Mitch circled to the landing where the stairs had been chopped out and stopped. "Pat, you worthless piece of manure! Damn it, I need matches."

He hurried back to the rooms and flung open the first door. He found the dresser and began feeling around in the drawers. Then he followed the bed to a toppled nightstand. The drawer was opened and he ran his hand through it, brushing a thick cobweb aside, shaking the stickiness from the backs of his fingers. He felt in it again and found a small box that rattled just right.

"Shoot," he swore happily, pocketing the matches and working his way to the window. "Gimmie the lantern," he called out to the woman. "Hurry it up. He's getting away."

Caroline, more than happy to be rid of

the distasteful, foul mouthed bandit, did her best to accommodate him, gathering the lantern and bringing it to his outstretched hand.

"You tell the others where I went if they come back, you hear me?"

"Fine," Caroline said and watched Mitch's head duck back into the window. *I'll let them know you went to hell*, she thought. She turned and looked down into the alley where that nice man Randy had fallen. She wasn't sure why she looked, or what she expected to see. Well, being honest with herself, she knew what she was looking for. She wanted to know if the poor man was really dead or just bitten. She knew what happened when someone got bit. She knew they would turn soon enough, change into a deader, and come up hungrier and more aggressive than the rest.

There wasn't much left of Randy's body. A few deaders gnawed at the remains like a pack of dogs. The others fought over scraps, a big limb dragged into the sage brush kept half a dozen of the deaders occupied. And then there were the sated ones, the two getting up from the kill with satisfied silence. They didn't struggle or fight with the others trying to vie for their spot. They just turned away.

"Dillon," Caroline gasped. She was certain it was her husband. She knew his tall, slender frame and the shortness of his hair, the youthful appearance of a clean shaven face. She knew by the length of his head, the breadth of his shoulders, and the stained white shirt he'd worn the last time she saw him.

"Come on, Suzanna," Caroline said while holding a hand out to let her daughter know they were going inside. "Quickly," she said, ushering the girl.

Mitch sat at the base of the stairs with the lantern beside him, fumbling for a match out of the box he'd found. He struck it once and nothing happened. He turned the box around and tried again. The match snapped and flared to life, igniting the room in shadow and white fire. He quickly lit the lantern, set the hood, and was about to climb down to the floor when he heard the woman calling out from above.

"Mister," she said. "We're coming with you."

"Huh?" Mitch said, looking up at her as she ushered her daughter along the balcony.

"I'll carry the lantern for you," she said. "So your hands are free to fight."

"Time's a wasting, lady," Mitch told her, climbing down to the saloon floor. "Keep up. If you fall behind, I'm taking the lantern and leaving you and your girl."

"Fair enough," she said breathlessly. She slid down beside him and helped her daughter climb down after. Mitch walked to the bar and put the lantern down, taking out his pistol to lead the way around behind it. Caroline picked up the axe under the landing and followed, handing the lantern to her daughter once they were both around the other side of the bar. "Well go on," she said. "Your man's getting away."

"I'm going, I'm going," Mitch growled, but didn't budge. "What do you suppose would happen if we close this trap door behind us? Can the deaders open it up?"

"I don't know," Caroline admitted.

"Sure worth a try," he said, stepping down onto the first step. "Come on, stay close."

Mitch walked them down to the basement to look around briefly, then turned back to pull the trap door shut from below. Its hinges squealed in protest and Mitch had to pull the door hard to get it to come down over the hole in the floor. The door slammed loudly over their heads. Caroline started from the noise, thinking that she had just sealed herself into her own tomb, but she would rather be dead than to see the likes of this mangy desperado kill her beloved husband, no matter what state he was in.

The basement smelled musty and the air, while being cooler, seemed heavier and harder to breath. Mitch checked the shadows, waving the other two to follow behind. Across from where the stairs touched the cellar floor was a cave mouth edged by wooden beams.

"That way, I suppose?" Mitch asked.

"Straight line all the way to the mines, then down."

"How the hell do the deaders fit through here?" Mitch asked, bending forward to fit in the low tunnel.

"The Chinamen fit fine," Caroline said. "All the rest…" she said, pointing at the ceiling. The cave passageway they followed had been carved out of the stone, leaving a nearly oval shape through which they passed. The ceiling was uneven and rough. Caught in virtually every protrusion was a tuft of hair where a deader had skimmed by.

"Serves 'em right," Mitch mumbled. He moved along slowly, excited and nervous about the prospect of what lay ahead. *They've all eaten already*, he reminded himself.

Sixteen

Jake hadn't seen anyone on top of the saloon since a light inside came on and then went out again. The moaners were no longer all jammed together in the alley between the saloon and the general store either. Quite a few had come out and were beginning to wander aimlessly toward the other buildings. Two stood at the doorway of the general store, another by its front window, all three facing inward. Jake wondered what he should do about that. He wished he could talk to one of the others. Should he shoot the moaners outside the store? What if Ben and Tucker were stuck in there and out of bullets? What if he tried to shoot the moaners, missed, and hit Ben or Tucker instead? Were they even inside anymore?

"Mitch!" Jake hollered one more time. "Randy!"

The only response was the endless drone of the moaners.

"Tuck!" he called out and waited. Still nothing.

"Ben!?"

He didn't like the notion of being alone. That's what got him in this pickle in the first place, following the goddamned Mexican rather than being alone. Well, he wasn't going to do it again, that was certain, and Baha got what was coming to him, sure enough. Still, laying on the floor boards of the hay loft, looking out over the town and its mindless inhabitants, he felt like a mouse stuck in its hole and hungry. He itched to get out of there and get going anywhere. Damned spirited mare of Ben's, rearing up on him like she did. If he hadn't let her go! She would have kicked him in the head for sure, he reasoned. When Randy's stallion bolted, all the others just tore themselves off the hitching post like it was a twig.

Jake rubbed his arm where he had been pulled against the hitching post, too stupid to let go of the reins. He was lucky he hadn't busted his arm. It hurt enough to feel like it had. He turned on his side to rest his shoulder, but felt something hard beneath him. He rolled off of it to feel around, fingering a round, leathery thing that was only big enough to fit in the palm of his hand. He brought it up to the trickling of light from the moon overhead to look at it, wondering what it could be. Being as hungry as he was it was easy to think of it as food, like a dried up peach. It was about the same size. When he turned it in the light, though, he shuddered, dropping the thing and shaking his fingers in the air, hoping he could shake off the disgust.

It was the ear the Mexican had been playing with, the one he'd just cut off that moaner earlier.

"Oh, dear God," Jake said and swept the back of his hand across the floor, flinging the ear out of the hayloft door. The Mexican had been holding it when he turned into one of those moaners. Now Jake had touched it too.

"Ben!" Jake shouted loudly, the panic in his voice apparent to even himself.

Please, Ben, answer me, Jake thought, closing his eyes hard, wishing he'd never touched that thing, wishing he'd just stayed on the first roof, wishing he'd never trusted Pat Ormsby.

"Oh, God, please don't let me become one of them things," he whispered.

"Ben!" he shouted again.

A gun shot erupted, muffled from being inside the general store, but Jake could see the flash of light when the shot went off, so he knew it had to be there.

"Damn it," Jake hissed, crooking his elbows and lifting the repeater to aim in the direction of the store. Another flash of light outlined the moaner in the front window. There were a number of other shadows inside, and Jake could make out the silhouette of Tucker or Ben, one of them for sure, shooting with a pistol raised high for good aim.

Jake took a deep, steadying breath and bore down the sights on the moaner in front of the window. Its arms were raised as it beat on the glass. It would get Ben and Tucker if they tried to run out the front.

Here's my chance, Jake thought, squeezing the trigger, hoping for redemption at last. The moaner jerked and crashed forward from the force of the bullet hitting it. Jake wasn't sure where he got him, square in the back, in the head, in the shoulder. It didn't matter all that much. What mattered was that he hit him.

The moaner slammed into the front window, shattering it with its two raised fists. The plates of glass glistened like stars for a moment, reflecting the moonlight as it toppled down and inward. The moaner fell into the store with it.

"Shoot," Jake cursed while cranking the repeater. He didn't think it would break out the glass! *Ah shoot, I've done it again*, he thought despairingly, angry with himself for making another mess of things. He still held a flicker of hope, though. He may have killed that last one. Maybe he was doing some good after all.

He moved his aim to the two moaners leaning against the front door. Unless Ben and Tucker were planning on coming out the window, they needed a clear path. He could fix that at least. He took in a deep breath again, took aim, and squeezed the trigger.

Seventeen

Ben stopped running his hand through the cabinet behind the counter and looked at the uneven floor board. He was certain he saw a light between the cracks. It wasn't enough to illuminate a room, hardly even equal to the glint of a star, but it ran the length of the uneven panel as though coming through the crack between two planks.

Ben knelt down and slipped his knife from his belt, using it to pry the edge of the board to loosen it. He could feel cool air coming up through the floor a little stronger than before. The boards chirped in protest, scraping against the tight confines of their socket.

"What's that?" Tucker whispered anxiously.

"I'm prying up the floor," Ben grunted.

"What the hell for?" Tucker hissed.

"Because there's light down there," Ben breathed, putting all his weight on the knife to try to pry the boards up. The flooring lifted out with a final groan and Ben fell backwards, knocking over several boxes that tumbled behind him with a heavy crash.

"Shoot," Ben swore. His back felt as though he'd fallen on the knife, but he still held it in his hand in front of him. Pain ran the length of his arm, remnants of his earlier fall. He managed to roll back onto his knees and lift the wooden floor boards up. The store was build a foot over the dirt, and directly beneath the opening in the floor was a hole in the ground about three feet around that went nearly straight down. A long ladder followed from about a foot below the hole all the way down to the bottom. It was lit from below with an orange glow that seemed to wander side to side, coming and going as though something big kept stepping in front of it and obscuring it. Ben could tell the bottom opened up into a bigger room or cavern.

"Look at this," Ben said to Tucker. Tucker was already half the way across the store by the time Ben stood up to try to move the wood trap door aside. "There's a light down there for sure."

"Don't let any moaners come up here!" Tucker groused, drawing his pistol as he came up around the open floor. He looked down with his pistol leading the way. "That's a long way down," he said.

"It's not even twenty feet," Ben told him.

"Well who's down there do you suppose? Do you think it's one of them moaners?"

"No. It's got to be someone…alive."

"Hey down there!" Tucker called down, holding his hand over his mouth. His voice echoed, not just into the hole, but through the store as well, bouncing off the high ceiling.

"What in the hell are you doing?" Ben snapped. He didn't want to fight his way out of the store again.

"Tuck?" a voice echoed back from down below.

"Mitch?" Tucker yelled into the hole. "Is that you?"

"How'd you get down here?" Mitch called back, his voice carrying his surprise.

"Hey, Mitch, do you see a ladder going up a hole?" Ben called down.

They heard another voice call out, "it's just ahead." It was the woman's voice. Both Ben and Tucker looked at one another.

"Is that that woman?" Ben called.

"I see the ladder now," Mitch said as way of answer. The light bobbed and grew brighter, widening the size of the cavern below them until a figure appeared and looked up. "Where you boys at?" Mitch called. His voice sounded like a cannon as it rose up from the depths.

"What are you doing down there?" Ben asked.

"Going after Ormsby. Where are you?"

"In the store, you nitwit," Tucker said.

"Where's Ormsby?" Ben called, slapping Tucker in the chest to get him to shut up.

"He came down here a few minutes ago, carrying Jake's satchel."

"Where's Randy?" Ben asked.

"He didn't make it," Mitch said solemnly, turning his head to look up and down the cave he was in. "You hear that moaning?" he asked, drawing his pistol.

Ben looked up at Tucker, then over toward the back door. There were at least three shadowy deaders shuffling in their direction. The groaning, now that they were paying attention to it, was so loud Ben could hardly think straight. He started to slip his knife back into its sheath so he could draw his pistol.

"Goddammit!" Tucker cursed, annoyed and frustrated at having been caught off guard. He drew his pistol and took aim at the nearest one. "Here," he said, pulling the trigger. "Eat some of this." The crack of the shot echoed throughout the store, the burst of light from the shot lighting up the moaner's eyes for a brief moment, long enough to let

Tucker know he missed hitting where he wanted. The moaner spun around and careened to the floor. That wouldn't kill him, though.

Tucker tried his luck with the next moaner, stepping sideways to get a better angle. Ben still held the trap door open, which was in the way of him getting close enough to the counter to see what happened to the first moaner he'd shot. He didn't want the thing crawling around the counter and grabbing at him in the dark.

Tucker shot again. The second moaner fell straight back, but Tucker hadn't hit him square either.

"Shoot, we need light," Tucker said hotly. "I can't see straight in here."

The front window crashed down as a moaner toppled through and both Ben and Tucker turned toward the sight, startled.

"What the?" Tucker asked, seeing several moaners shambling in the street beyond. "We're trapped," he announced.

"We ain't trapped," Ben said. Tucker took another shot at the nearest moaner as it tried to rise again. The front door rattled heavily as he did, as though one of the other moaners had thrown itself at the door. The echo of a gunshot exhaled from somewhere outside. "Get in here."

"Down there?" Tucker asked, waving

his pistol at the hole. Another blast went off and both Tucker and Ben ducked.

"Someone's shooting from outside!" Tucker exclaimed.

"Get in the hole," Ben insisted.

"Good idea," Tucker said, slipping his pistol into his holster and stepping down to the dirt, hoping there weren't any snakes hiding in the shadows under the store. He had to trust his foot would catch the ladder. There wasn't anything to hold onto as he crouched and slid his feet into the hole. Ben fired his pistol at the nearest deader that was beginning to reach over the countertop toward him. Behind that deader there were at least three others coming in through the open back door. Another gun blast from outside rang out.

"Get down the hole, dammit," Ben shouted, stepping into the hole beside Tucker's hands.

"This ain't easy!" Tucker shouted back, feeling for the next rung with his foot. Ben leaned around the trap door that he propped up with his shoulder to see movement on the floor, something crawling. He fired at it, but in the darkness he hardly even slowed it down.

Ben crouched down over Tucker and felt the burn in his spine.

"Shoot," he groaned as his legs gave

out from under him. He fell onto Tucker with the weight of the trap door pressing on his back. His feet slid into the hole and dragged over Tucker's back.

"Get off me!" Tucker yelled.

"Son of a…" Ben began to swear. Fire lanced up and down his spine and he arched his head back, banging the back of his head on the trap door above. It felt loose. Ben had sense enough to reach an arm up and push it, to try to slide it into place. With the last bit of strength he could muster he shoved the trapdoor into the air and it fell again, thumping into place.

"Get your goddamned knees out of my back," Tucker insisted as he wedged himself out from under Ben's weight. Ben's elbows kept him from sliding further into the hole. Tucker had kept the rest of him from falling straight down. Ben hardly had the strength to slip his feet into the rungs as Tucker descended below him. Instead he lay on his belly and tried not to move. He hoped it would help subside the pain. Above him he heard the closeness of a deader's moan, the way it inhaled with a deep, raspy hiss before protesting the barrier between them. Its fingers scratched at the wood and Ben wondered if the things would be able to figure it out and come down after them sooner or later.

"You coming?" Tucker asked as he

made his way down the ladder.

Eighteen

There hadn't been anymore gunshots.

"Ben!?" Jake yelled out desperately. "Tucker?! Any of you other fellas out there? Randy? Mitch!?"

There was still no response except the groaning and moaning rising from town.

"Jesus, Lady, are you even still there?" he shouted.

Again no answer.

Where'd they all go, he wondered?

Jake shivered. What if they'd all become moaners? He'd shot three of the moaners out in front of the general store, and then some more in the street, but none of them stayed down for long. Even all the ones he'd shot in the street rescuing Baha had gotten right back up. Shooting them didn't kill them, but it certainly lamed them up a bit. Jake saw one of the moaners he'd just shot listing to the side as it dragged its left leg instead of picking it up proper. Another one of the moaners didn't lift its right arm when it came to a wall like the rest did. He'd watched several throughout the night. They'd reach a wall and act dumbstruck, looking it up and down. They'd beat on the wall at first, then they'd drag their nails down it as though they might somehow claw through something as big as a building. *What a bunch of stupid idiots*, Jake thought.

He sat up and picked out more bullets for the repeater, loading it carefully in the dark. What he wouldn't give for a horse right about now, even Ben's damned mare. If only he'd held onto her bridle. She would have broken his arm, but maybe she would have dragged him off into the desert with her, someplace far away from here. He could have lived with that, a broken arm and ten miles. That was enough for safety, he figured.

"Ben!?" he called out and waited, but heard no response. He'd try every so often. He had nothing else to do.

Nineteen

"Would you two keep it down?" Mitch snapped, his voice muffled by Tucker's body between them in the hole. Tucker had only moved down a few steps since getting unstuck from Ben, but he had complained with every slow, painful rung of the ladder. "You stepped on my hand, Ben," was the first thing he complained about. That hardly hurt compared to his leg. "How am I supposed to shoot without my good hand?"

"You ain't so good a shot anyway," Ben had managed to reply through gritted teeth.

"You're one to talk."

"Hush up," the woman snapped from below and both Tucker and Ben stopped where they were on the ladder to look down. "There're deaders down here, for Christ sake!"

"Then what the hell we going down there for?" Tucker mumbled up to Ben.

"Just climb down," Ben sighed. It was a better fate to try to find a way out down below than to instead wait for the deaders over his head to surely figure out a way through the floor boards.

Ben had to lead each step down with his left foot because of the pain when he shifted his weight the other direction. He'd get a good bearing of where the next rung should be and then just drop off the one above, using his arms to ease him to a landing. Tucker wasn't faring much better given how slowly he was descending ahead of him.

Tucker made an effort to pat the dirt and dust off of himself at the bottom, waiting quietly after that with the others. Ben slid down the last few rungs of the ladder to stand on solid ground with his unsteady legs.

"What happened to Randy?" Ben asked.

Mitch grimaced and shook his head. "Same as you," Mitch whispered. "Fell off the roof. Deaders all got him. Tore him to pieces, Ben. It was…I dunno. I ain't never seen the likes of it."

Ben looked at the woman, Caroline if he remembered right. She closed her eyes to block out the memory of it. Ben knew there was more to it than that. He figured he needed to keep an eye on both Tucker *and* Mitch now.

"Did I hear right? Was Jake shooting at the two of you?" Mitch whispered. "He's got Baha's repeater and all his ammunition. He said he killed the Mexican."

"Well he's up there and we're down here, so we'll worry over him later," Ben said. "What's the plan?"

"Plan?"

"You know, for going after Ormsby. What did you have in mind?"

"Well, I was gonna follow him to his hole, shoot him in the back, and take the satchel."

"That's it?" Tucker asked in disbelief.

"He just came down a few minutes ago. He's just up ahead for sure."

"Lady, you came down here with this nitwit?" Tucker asked her.

"Would you put a lid on it, Tuck?" Ben asked.

"That wouldn't even work," Tucker sputtered. "You got to shoot 'em in the head or they just get back up."

"Then I'll shoot him in the back of the head!" Mitch snapped.

"Fellas, shut it!" Ben growled. He side stepped toward Caroline, glancing her way to see if she was distressed. She held an axe across her front with both hands, he eyes narrow and grim. Her daughter, the deaf one named Suzanna, held the lantern by her side. Her young eyes looked perplexed by the conversation. Luckily, Ben thought, she couldn't hear a word of it. "Which way did

Ormsby go?"

Caroline nodded the direction as Mitch pointed down the same long, dark passageway. At least they were in agreement, but Ben wanted to know what she was doing down here in the first place. The passage curved, dipping down like a long, empty prairie fading in the distance. Ben looked back the other way, where Mitch had come from.

"What about deaders coming from down there?" Ben asked with a nod of his chin.

"I closed the trap door behind us," Mitch said.

"That ain't going to hold them long," Ben and Tucker said in unison, the only difference was the level of disgust in their tones.

"Did you bar it from underneath?" Tucker asked. His tone left no doubt he didn't trust Mitch to make a sound decision.

"Would you quit it with acting like I'm stupid?" Mitch snapped.

"No," Caroline said, surprising everyone. "There ain't a way to bar it from below."

"Then we'll need to keep an eye out both ways," Ben said. "I'll bring up the rear. Who wants to lead?"

"Shoot, it's his idea," Tucker said, waving his pistol toward Mitch.

"Fine," Mitch shrugged, stepping past the others. "Just keep up."

"Do you know what's up ahead?" Ben asked Caroline.

"It's just a long passageway. It goes on for half a mile, then splits. The old path heads to the right. The new mine, where I think all the dead came from, is to the left. It's steep going down there, but they cut stairs in to it."

"Got it. Go left at the split," Mitch said, taking several bold strides toward the darkness. Tucker began to follow him. Caroline and the girl didn't move.

"What's wrong?" Tucker asked sharply. "Come on."

"If you find my husband down there you leave him be, otherwise you can just carry on from here on your own."

"What?" Tucker hissed.

"Tuck," Ben warned. "We may need her to find our way."

"We got all night to find our way. How big can this mine be?"

"I'd rather not find out," Ben insisted.

"I ain't gonna let a moaner bite me to death on account she's still wishful thinking," Tucker declared.

"Alright, then good luck finding your way down there," Caroline said, turning and reaching a hand for her daughter.

"Miss," Ben said apologetically, holding a hand for her to stay. "Don't go running off now. We promise not to kill your husband if we find him down here, but we may have to tie him up or something."

"With what?" Tucker laughed with disbelief. He stepped closer to Caroline, asking, "Is it all right if we shoot him in the leg instead of killing him?"

"When we find him, I'll take care of him," she said grimly, hefting the axe.

"That's fair enough, ma'am," Ben said, not so sure her mettle matched her resolve. "I already said we'd do it."

"Well then why doesn't she get out in front so we know which one of 'em is her husband?"

Ben didn't like the idea on a number of levels. For one, she was a woman, and besides that, he would much rather see Mitch or Tucker out front if one of those deaders lunged up out of the shadows.

"That ain't gonna be necessary," Ben replied. "We'll all stay close, alright?"

"Fine," Tucker grumbled. "Let's just get Ormsby and get the hell out of here before morning. There *is* another way out, ain't there?" Tucker asked Caroline.

"There're two," she said.

Everyone eyed her, even her deaf

daughter, though the girl looked more perplexed about what was going on than from understanding anything of what was being said.

It made Ben nervous to think of another hole. He knew there must be a way to the surface at the destroyed campsite. What bothered him is where the other hole might be, and if it was covered right now.

Twenty

The wide brim of the Mexican's sombrero lurched into the open. Jake sat up straight at the sight.

"Baha?" he asked. He couldn't believe his eyes. The Mexican was dead. Jake had shot him in the chest with his own damned repeater. What's more, he'd fallen from the loft. He shouldn't be walking, even as stiff legged and awkwardly as he was. He should be dead.

The Mexican took one step, lurching ahead, planting a foot hard and purposefully. The sombrero swayed a moment. Then the next leg pitched forward, threatening to topple the heavy Mexican, but again the foot came down with a stomp and his head beneath the sombrero swayed.

"Why won't none of you die?" Jake asked. The Mexican stopped and craned his head. Jake heard the throaty moan from his ex-partner. Even his moan sounded like a different language. The large Mexican's body began to pivot, turning around as though spinning on a single peg leg planted firmly in a hole.

"Why ain't you dead?" Jake demanded,

raising the repeater. "I shot you!"

The Mexican moaned in response, his empty eyes realizing the source of the sound. Baha took one jerky step forward.

"No you don't," Jake said, leaning into the sights of the repeater. "You go to hell where you belong!"

He pulled the trigger. The riffle kicked against his shoulder just as the impact of the bullet staggered the Mexican backwards. The Mexican didn't fall. Jake sneered, cranking the repeater and settling it to his shoulder to sight him again.

He fired and Baha staggered forward on an unsteady leg.

"Ha," Jake yelled. "Try walking with no knees!"

He cranked the repeater again and drew down his aim once more.

The Mexican lifted himself from his hands and knees. He tried to lift one leg but lost balance and fell forward again. Jake watched with shock as Baha, a determined and unrelenting vessel that defied the bounds of nature Jake knew and understood, threw himself upright again and lifted his other knee in an attempt to stand.

Jake glowered and shut one eye to take aim, pulling the trigger once more.

Baha's raised knee collapsed sideways

just as he began to stand. He slumped forward once more, landing face first in the dirt street. He didn't stir for a moment. Jake cranked the repeater with satisfaction.

"Try and eat my foot?" Jake sneered. "That'll learn you."

The sombrero lifted and arms spread out, pushing the heavy Mexican upright onto all fours. In the dim light Jake couldn't tell the significance of the wounds he'd already inflicted, but by all rights the man should have been dead twice over. The sombrero lifted further, revealing the outline of the man beneath.

"Now, if maybe I can knock that sombrero off of your head," Jake began, closing an eye to take aim.

Twenty-One

Their own shadows led the way into darkness. Every ten or twenty paces the passageway narrowed between two beams that held up a heavy cross beam. The orange glow from the lantern the girl carried went as far as the beams, but refused to prowl any further into the blackness beyond. Mitch lifted his hat, wiping the cold sweat from his forehead before running his fingers through his slick blond hair. He stopped, slipping the hat on again, waiting for the others to get closer. If the light wouldn't go in there, he reckoned, why should he?

"Why you stopping again?" Tucker whispered.

"Why is that girl so God awful slow?" Mitch hissed. He turned around, whispering, "hold it out to the side!" He wasn't talking to the little girl. She couldn't hear a damned thing anyone said. The woman picked her daughter's hand up. The light worked its way around the woman, Tucker, and Mitch to light enough of the way ahead that Mitch wasn't as afraid to step past the big beams. He led with his pistol, checking the shadows left and right, expecting a deader to be standing there, waiting to lunge out at him.

"How much further?" Mitch whispered back.

"Just a few more" the woman replied.

"You already said that," Mitch grumbled.

"Then why don't you try walking faster?" Tucker asked softly.

Mitch didn't say anything. Tucker was an ass. Jawing with him never amounted to anything but a jaw ache. Mitch reached the next set of beams and waited, again unable to see anything but the shadows creeping forward, growing bigger and darker, consuming him and what little light there was. Images of the deaders falling over Randy kept surfacing in his mind. He looked back even though he knew it was Tucker and the others following him. He saw shadowy outlines, Tucker's face especially shrouded in a veil of black that obscured everything except his eyes. Then the lantern light reached around them and half of Tucker's face glowed with a recognizable, irritable expression.

"Any time," Tucker whispered, motioning ahead.

"Tell that to the girl," Mitch grumbled under his breath. He stepped through the narrow beams, gun leading the way, focused on the shadows that seemed poised to leap upon him. With so many shadows, he hardly looked to the ground. He kicked something and nearly stumbling over it. He spun around, taking a leap further into the passageway as he pointed his pistol at the object on the ground.

Tucker stopped and sank low, his pistol raised in alarm.

The woman gasped and pulled the girl close.

The light swung across the passage, stretching the shadows on one side while slashing them from the other.

"What is it?" Ben whispered fiercely.

"Something on the ground," Mitch said before Ben was finished.

Caroline took the lantern from her daughter and lifted it high in the passageway. Tucker blanched at the sight of it, a hand with several fingers gnawed partly off, stretches of flesh missing, the remnants of a shirt sleeve stretched out from the wrist as long as a whole arm, but partly empty as though only half the forearm still filled the fabric. Filthy, bloody stains covered the loose sleeve.

"What in the..." Tucker asked, managing to suppress the rest of his thought.

"Well?" Ben asked.

"It's a hand," Tucker replied

"A hand?" Ben asked.

"Randy's," Mitch replied, clearly shaken by the sight.

Tucker stood and kicked the hand off to the side of the cave. The long, empty shirtsleeve, still bound at the wrist, went with it, lying beside it like empty snake skin. As revolting as it was, he fought off a shudder and kicked dirt over it to try to hide it more. He wasn't thinking of the woman or the child. The last thing he would ever admit was that it was just plain unsettling to look at, the way the fingers had been chewed off and the remaining flesh drug off the bone.

"Keep going," Tucker whispered as steadily as he could. Mitch glared at him fiercely. Tucker stepped closer to Mitch, stepping between him and the severed hand to block the sight of it. Tucker swallowed hard. "Keep a move on. I'm right behind you."

Mitch took a deep, steadying breath and turned around.

"I'm right here," Tucker said again, hoping his show of strength was enough to encourage the rest of them to get as far from this place as possible. He began wondering where this other way out of the mines might be.

Twenty-Two

Ben stepped past the mound of partially buried flesh, gazing down at it with remorse. The tattered and filthy shirt sleeve could have been anyone's. Just because Mitch said it was Randy's didn't make it so. It could have been any of the deaders hands from any one they'd shot, but still, not knowing what happened to Randy made him uncomfortable looking at the severed hand. A shiver ran up his spine.

Having to look back over and over to make sure nothing was sneaking up on them as they walked down the passageway didn't make it any easier. Every time he looked back he saw the lump. With what he'd seen so far, a part of him expected the hand to start clawing its way after them. He shook his head to rid himself of such thoughts.

The other trouble that plagued him was the stabbing pains in his leg and back. If he could just lay down for a little while, he thought.

The woman glanced back at him every so often. Something about her had changed since coming down here. Up on the roof she had been satisfied just quietly waiting out the night, but down here she had become darker than the shadows, a fierceness growing with each step they took deeper into the earth. It was in the way she treated her daughter, the way her knuckles clutched the handle of the axe. Unlike the rest of them, she knew what was ahead. She was expecting something bad to happen.

Ben was too. Maybe it was the confined spaces that had him on edge. The passage was so narrow that his shoulders brushed against the support beams in some places. It was built by Chinamen for sure. He wondered how Pat Ormsby had come through, or how any of the townsfolk had. He wondered how they found their way in the pitch black.

"Do you smell that?" Tucker asked, breaking a long silence. Ben wondered how many of those hundred feet they'd travelled.

"Yeah," Mitch replied. "Like rotten eggs. You suppose that's the deaders?"

"It's sulfur," the woman said. "From the gas leak."

"You mean we're already there?" Mitch asked, stopping.

"No, it's everywhere in the mine now. It gets stronger the closer you get."

That answered something – at least Ben figured the deaders used that smell of sulfur to find their way in the dark. He and his gang could do the same. They probably didn't need the woman after all, but Ben thought it best not to mention it to the others. None of the outcomes of making his thoughts known were good for her or her daughter, and Ben just didn't have the stomach for turning her loose on her own, nor killing her.

"The closer you get to what?" Ben asked. Everyone looked back at him, even the little girl who was following eyes.

"Dillon called it the gas chamber," the woman answered. "The night he led the first group down here to…kill the dead, that's when he found it. He told me about it when he came back with only some of the others."

"Hold it, I thought you said you never saw him again," Mitch put in. Ben was thinking the same.

"That was before he turned. He'd been bitten but tried to hide it. I think he believed he could cure it, or that it didn't affect everyone, or something." Caroline shook her head, closing her eyes to fend off the memory.

"Let's stop jawing about it and get Pat and get the hell out of here," Tucker said. "There can't be but a half dozen or so moaners down here. I say we shoot them all – with the exception of your dearly departed, of course," he added with mock sincerity.

"Let's divvy up the ammo first," Mitch suggested.

"Easy for you to say," Tucker objected. "You've only got but six rounds left on that belt of yours."

"Looks like you're sporting a dozen."

"Would you two hush?" Ben admonished. "Mitch, if I give you another six of mine will you be quiet?"

Mitch didn't answer.

"Here, ma'am," Ben said, holding out a fist full of bullets. "Pass these up to Mitch." Caroline obliged. Ben stood still and listened to the darkness, hearing only the breathing of the others and the bullets clicking together in Mitch's hand as he slid them into his belt straps one by one. He felt a soft, slow breeze across his neck, cooling his sweaty skin.

He took a book of matches from his pocket and lit one. The flame hissed to life, its smoke pouring sidelong back the way they had come, the flame wobbling and bending in the same direction.

"Where's that other way out?" Ben asked, holding the match up for Caroline to see it.

"It ain't behind us if that's what you're thinking," she said. "That hole you came down is where the air's leading. That and the cellar of the saloon. The buildings are all raised, so just because the doors are closed doesn't mean the air's stuck too."

Ben dropped the match.

"Go on, Mitch," Ben whispered. "Let's get to that intersection."

They squeezed between eight more sets of beams and they were there. The smaller cave they had been in opened up into a wider passageway where they could stand two abreast. A narrow gauge track in the ground lead up a long, gentle looking cave that sloped and curved out of sight toward where Ben knew the campsite to be. Ben lit another match and watched the flame bend in the same direction, toward the campsite. It confirmed what he was thinking, that the other way out was likely further down in the mines.

The other direction came to an end in a large, dug out cave. A single, half-full rail cart was parked there. All over the floor were canvas rags, mostly just empty and strewn about, some filled with mounds of rocks and dirt. Ben had seen Chinamen use flat cloth like this before. They laid them out, shoveled dirt and rocks on top, then picked up the four corners to haul it off. It was easier and faster than using sacks. He sure had to hand it to the Chinamen for coming up with such good, simple ideas.

They fanned out in the room, the

woman and her daughter standing next to the rail cart, waiting for Ben and the others to look in all the shadowy crevices. Ben shuffled sideways along the wall, pointing his pistol into every shadow, expecting something to stir, something to lurch out at him.

"Hey," Tucker whispered, startling Ben. He looked over his shoulder to where Tucker was standing. "There's another cave here," Tucker pointed with a wave of his pistol. "It goes down."

"That's the way," Caroline said solemnly.

"There's a box of candles over here," Mitch said softly. "A couple dozen at least."

They each lit one and started down the passageway in the same order as before. The new cave had long flat stairs carved into the ground spaced irregularly, making it hard to go down quickly. It was wide enough for two Chinamen to pass one another, but not for the others to walk side-by-side. With each step, Ben's candle threatened to blow itself out, sputtering sideways.

"Shoot," Tucker hissed just before his candle blew itself out. "Goddamned hot wax!"

Ben dipped his candle forward to drain off some hot wax from the top to avoid burning himself like Tucker had. After that they all walked slower. No one wanted to be without their own light.

"Here," Ben said, touching the back of his hand to the woman's arm. Caroline looked down and he held out a box of matches. "In case the lantern goes out." She took the matches and shoved them into her pocket without a word.

"Where the hell is this chamber?" Mitch whispered back as he came to a stop, leaning against the wall to let the light of the lantern past him. They had come down nearly a hundred steps already. "And how the hell do the deaders see where they're going?"

"They don't need to see," Tucker answered softly. "That smell is getting worse."

The sulfuric scent in the air was far more pungent down here, taking on an acrid bite. Ben sniffed at it a few times and scowled. As he stood still he watched the candle flame bend with the breeze washing up from ahead. He turned to look behind him, grimacing as a spike of pain drove up his spine. Damn it if his back wasn't getting worse with pain! These stairs were hardly helping. Luckily there was nothing behind them but darkness. *If they could just lay down a minute to rest*, he thought.

"Keep going," the woman insisted. "It's just a little further."

Mitch mumbled something but kept

moving, holding a hand in front of his candle to keep it from blowing out. They walked toward the edge of darkness as it grew wider and taller. The chamber they found had numerous passages that split off in several directions.

"Alright," Mitch whispered as he plucked his pistol out again, turning in every direction. "Which one of these is the way?"

Ben fished a silver dollar from his pocket and dropped it on the ground at the mouth of the cave passageway they had come through. His candle began dancing back and forth now, as though the mines were alive and breathing. The smell of sulfur had changed even more. Now there was a pungent and metallic smell, as though he were tasting his own blood through his nose, like he did after losing a fist fight. And there was something else…rot.

"Well?" Tucker asked the woman.

She pulled her daughter closer to her side. Ben stepped up beside her, looking down at the deaf girl, Suzanna, who stared up at her mother questioningly. Caroline looked down with a soothing smile, putting a hand on the girl's cheek. The girl turned her head into her mother's hand and took hold of it with both hands.

The woman didn't answer.

Ben held his flickering candle in front of her. The flame bent one direction, hissed and flickered as it tried to straighten, then turned and bent another way.

"You don't know, do you?" Ben asked softly.

"Oh, Jesus, are you kidding me?" Mitch said exasperated.

"I think it's that one," she said, pointing. The hole she pointed at looked no different than the others except for the worn path leading into it seemed more recently used. "I know the other exit is there. That's where the cave-in was. Dillon never told me--"

"The cave in?" Ben interrupted.

"Before they all started dying," Caroline whispered. Ben could tell she was clearly distressed being down here, which made him wonder why she had come at all. He hated not being able to trust anyone. Not his own gang, and now most certainly not her.

Twenty-Three

"Twenty or so of the Chinamen were trapped on the other side of the cave-in wall," Caroline explained. "The others and some of the townsfolk, Dillon included, worked to clear the way back to them. I came down here a few times with food and water for Dillon.

"We couldn't clear the tunnel that caved-in. Every time we dug some out, it collapsed again. The Chinamen on the other side ran into the same trouble, but they were smart. It was a wet, soft vein that caused it all, so while we were digging for them, they dug sideways to another tunnel and came out behind us."

"Were they digging for silver or that new element when they had that cave-in?" Ben asked, leaning against a wall between two cave passages. He needed to lie down, but based on the constant pain he was in now he figured he likely wouldn't have been able to get back up.

"I don't know," she said, shaking her head.

"So the cave-in is another way out. How's that?" Ben asked.

"Each time they dug it up, it collapsed some more until there was an air vent. It's a crack going at an angle straight up to the hillside about a half mile past the miner's cave entrance. Dillon and some of the Chinamen went through it."

"So why do you think this one's where the gas chamber is?" Tucker asked from his perch next to the cave entrance to the one she'd pointed out earlier.

"They started digging in there again right after the cave-in. When they started digging again, that's when the dead came back to life."

"Alright, that's good enough for me," Ben said. "Let's give it a try before any deaders come up from behind."

"Before we go," Caroline said sharply. "I've got to warn you. Don't breathe the gas. Don't lay down in there. Don't even touch the walls."

"All well and good advice, but then how're we supposed to fish out Ormsby?" Tucker asked. He held up his candle to his face and covered it with a hand as he started into the passageway. "Next you're gonna say don't even light a match, or something. Come on, Mitch. We're wasting time."

Mitch glanced toward Ben for a moment and Ben nodded to go on.

"Come on, Miss," Ben said reluctantly, stepping away from the wall he'd been resting against. His back felt the fire of each step. He took a spare candle out of his pocket and tossed it to the mouth of the passage that led to the cave-in. *Just in case*, he thought.

The passage gradually rose rather than descending into the hillside. The smell was still heavy in the air, but when Ben paused to let his candle flame show the direction of air, the candle went still except for the unsteadiness of his hand. The ground began to take on a strange, almost distorted appearance, as though the others had kicked up dust with their boots that simply hadn't settled yet. The air itself felt heavier, although Ben reasoned it was just the stillness of it and his nerves getting to him.

The passage turned ahead and Tucker and Mitch disappeared around its edge. As each did the light of their candles traced its way around the edge of the cave in the opposite direction, as though the whole of it were mirrors or glass. Ben blinked away the effect, rubbing his eyes with the back of his hand. The same thing happened as he came around the bend with Caroline close ahead. The light of Mitch's candle, then of Tuckers, appeared to their right, then swung around the cave both to the top and bottom to appear to their left where the two men stood, holding their candles above their heads with their pistols drawn, pointing ahead of them where only blackness stood.

Caroline sucked in a breath and stopped in her tracks. Ben looked at her as he stepped around her and her girl. Caroline held Suzanna against her belly in a tight, motherly grip. Caroline's eyes were wide in fear.

"It'll be alright," Ben whispered as softly as he could, plucking out his pistol and stepping past her. He moved up to the edge of whatever precipice the other two stood at, his candle leading the way, flickering only from his own movement. The air was so still it hardly seemed possible to breathe it in. He took one long, steadying breath as he reached the top.

The cave sloped down ahead of them into an enormous cavern that was studded above and below with stalactites and stalagmites of different sizes, which glistened as though encrusted with gem stones from the candle's reflection. At his feet and filling the room as far as their candle light reached, which wasn't nearly as far as the darkness beyond, it looked as though a pool of undulating, putrid water had formed. It wasn't water, Ben realized. It crept over the lip of the ground where they stood to pour gently down the tunnel, fanning out as it did, dissipating from a visible form into the obscuring look of the ground where the woman and her daughter stood anchored a few paces back. The light of the lantern filled the passageway behind them to the bend.

"That's a lot more gas than I figured," Mitch whispered, his words barely breaking the silence.

"You ever see anything like this?" Tucker asked, equally soft.

Ben shook his head. Even the sound of skin chafing the neck of his jacket seemed too loud for this place. Ben tapped a toe into the gas in the room, disrupting it gently. Like water it gave, sucking back to fill the void when he moved his boot back. Unlike water, though, the rest of the pool didn't seem to stir. This stuff was much heavier, far slower, than water.

"So what do we do?" Tucker asked, still barely loud enough to be heard.

Ben didn't have an answer. Up until now he had hoped things would be easier, that Tucker or Mitch would see Pat and shoot him, and that would be that. He lowered his candle to get a better look at the lake of gas. It was yellow, thick as smoke, but so heavy it rested on the ground instead of rising like gases were supposed to.

"Don't touch it," Mitch warned him.

"He already did, dumb-ass," Tucker

replied at something below a whisper. "And we're all standing in it already!"

"Just don't light it on fire. It'll blow us all to kingdom come."

"No, it won't," Tucker said.

"And don't call me a dumb-ass," Mitch warned. "Anyway, how are we gonna find Pat in all this?"

Ben didn't even want to find Pat Ormsby anymore.

"I'll tell you how," Tucker said, removing his hat. He took a gentle, slow step down into the gas and firmly planted his foot in it. He looked at both Ben and Mitch with a triumphant smirk. *Look who's yellow bellied now*, Tucker thought. He stepped the other foot forward into the room and planted it as well, then fanned the ground with his hat. The gas swirled and roiled, bubbling and washing away from his feet and he took three bold and quick steps forward before the yellow cloud settled back in over the emptiness. It swirled from behind, snaking between his legs.

"I don't think we should stir it up like that," Mitch whispered. "Besides," he added, crouching down with the candle to see the gas reforming again. The ground faded and turned yellow once more as though the gas were seeping up from the very earth. "That still won't help you see where Ormsby's hiding."

"Shut it," Tucker mumbled, fanning the gas with his hat again. He pushed through the trough and waded further into the chamber. This wasn't so frightening, even though the gas was getting deeper. At first it hardly reached the tops of his boots, but now it was higher than his knees. He looked back to see Ben and Mitch still standing at the mouth of the passage, the light from behind making them into partial shadows of themselves, their candles lighting only their faces. He looked ahead at the endless darkness, squinting to see past his own light. He moved his candle to his side to see better. The chamber had an end. He could see it, but it was a long way off. The stalagmites shrank in height ahead, getting so small they barely protruded through the surface at all just another ten paces. That would put the gas up to his waist.

"I'm going to need more light," Tucker whispered behind him. "Get that lantern up here."

He fanned at the gas again and took several quick steps into the roiling cloud. The smells that mixed in the air got progressively worse. The sulfuric scent was thick but also a musty rot had grown, and to make things worse, it smelled of tin. That's what blood smelled like to him.

He fanned the gas as he moved side to

side, not bothering to stop anymore. The pool of heavy gas was up to his thighs now, and even fanning it aside he hardly saw the ground beneath him any longer. He let his arm down, too tired to hold the candle much higher anymore. A dark shape formed in the gas, a long shadow that lay sprawled in front of him. He fanned his hat gently, waving away the top layers of the gas until the form took shape. He sucked in his breath at the sight of a moaner, a Chinaman laying on the ground face up with his eyes closed. Tucker stuffed his hat under his other armpit and drew his pistol.

We probably should have tried making a racket first, Tucker thought, taking aim at the sleeping moaner's head.

Blam!

The noise erupted like a hundred cannon firing from the deck of a sailing vessel. The gas clouds all around him lit up as though shots were repeating in every direction, as though his bullet were ricocheting off every stalagmite under the pool of gas.

Tucker stared down the length of the cavern as the light danced and wove throughout the immense cavern.

"Oh, shoot," he muttered, realizing that the light wasn't from a bullet, but instead fire touching off in every pocket of gas across the surface of the lake of yellow. It wasn't flat as he'd thought, but instead uneven like the ripples on a lake in wind, each trough filled now with a ball of blue flame turning in on itself, diving under the waves, erupting elsewhere, racing every which way, but most importantly, coming back at him at amazing speed. He shrugged, holding an arm over his face as it charged. He couldn't outrun this.

"Tuck!" he heard Mitch gasp just as the flames surged past.

He expected to be dead, or at the very least horribly burned, but even as the eddies of blue fire continued to wash over him this way and that he felt nothing. The room was lit by a thousand candles, though, and the moist walls and ceiling shimmered and glistened like diamonds.

"Jesus H. Christ, Ben, look at it all lit up like that," Mitch whispered. "Do you think we died and that's the road to heaven?"

"None of us were going to heaven," Ben replied. "The gas is on fire, is all."

"I'm not burnt," Tucker said, looking again into the ocean of undulating flame. The blue wisps of fire danced at his legs, swimming by and climbing like tiny waves breaking against sturdy rocks. Tucker put his hand out to feel the flames, to gauge how hot it was. "It don't hurt," he called back.

A hand gripped him, and not his own.

It took him by the ankle and tugged, but his boot caught on the rough ground and helped him keep his footing. His arms waved erratically, dashing the candle light and causing his hat to fall into the gas. The form beneath the surface was obscured, just some large thing that swam closer to his other leg.

Tucker caught his balance and aimed his pistol again, hoping that the narrower end closest to him was the moaner's head. In the flaming soup undulating beneath him he couldn't tell.

Blam! He shot once. The grip slackened and he kicked the hand off of himself.

"Tuck?" Mitch called.

"I'm all right. I must have missed that moaner the first time," Tucker said, then took a deep breath and blew downward to try to see its head. He couldn't blow enough of the gas aside, and the pocket he created only grew brighter with fire, forcing him to back away further.

Tucker turned and started walking out of the pool of fiery gas.

"Hey, Ben, I'm gonna need your hat."

Twenty-Four

"I told you, just shoot them in the side of the head," Tucker explained. "Right above the ear. Or right above or between the eyes."

Mitch didn't seem too keen on the idea of following Tucker into the burning gas chamber. This was nothing like what he had envisioned when he started chasing Pat Ormsby down here. He had even convinced himself that Ormsby might not have even come in here in the first place. Maybe the fat cuss had gotten lost and was wandering the other mine shafts.

"They twitch a lot if you do it right," Tucker added as he stepped into the pool of undulating fire. The bursts of blue flame had subsided a little, but pockets seemed to keep bubbling up everywhere. The brightest were toward the middle along the wall. Tucker wanted him to look there first. Everywhere Tucker stepped churned up blue fire.

Mitch looked back to where Ben was standing guard behind them with the woman and the girl. That was an easy job. Why couldn't he have had that? Of course he knew why. Ben and Tucker didn't trust him. Well, the feeling was mutual, except with Ben there by the woman he knew he wasn't going to take the lantern and run off like he figured Tucker would, or how Ben might have been thinking Mitch would. That was what it boiled down to. It had nothing to do with hats.

Reluctantly Mitch followed Tucker into the gas chamber, giving a try at waving his hat to create pockets to see through. It worked fairly well, though the deeper he went, the more control he needed to fan his hat just right to swish aside the right amount of gas. Too much and the hole he made burst into white flame that felt hot. Too little and the pocket of blue that he made didn't reach the ground.

Before he knew it he was wading through the gas up to his thighs, which was an unsettling feeling. He followed in Tucker's wake rather than forging his own path, figuring that any deaders would grab hold of Tucker to warn them of their presence. Tucker had said he would be able to see them, though. He said they appeared as shadows, like enormous, dark fish just lurking under the surface, still as stones. None of those descriptions gave Mitch any comfort. He hated the water. He couldn't swim.

"Tuck," Mitch whispered, pointing toward a shadow to their right.

"What're you doing behind me?" Tucker hissed. "Go around along the far wall like I told you."

"But there's one of them shadow stones," Mitch struggled to whisper. His throat was tense out of fear, constricting his words.

"That's the one I shot already," Tucker dismissed with a wave of Ben's hat. "Shoot, Mitch, if you're not going to help, at least try to find my hat or something."

Mitch stopped following Tucker, letting him wade ahead. Tucker's head scanned the depths as he fanned the fog at his legs. The blue fire leapt and danced eerily, as though ghosts were swirling around him, clawing at his trousers to find some way into his body. Mitch looked down at the blue pockets of flame that lit up and disappeared in the undulating yellow gas beneath him. The blue swells cast a green pall over the gas around it. Mitch thought it looked like some slumbering ghost breathing quietly.

"Go on," Tucker whispered, looking back. He waved his pistol toward the other wall. "They're sleeping or something. They've got their eyes closed and everything."

So he says, Mitch thought. Tucker had only seen one deader in the pool of fog. Who was to say that it was the only sleeper in the bunch? What if maybe the rest of them heard the gun shots and were hiding, waiting for their chance to leap up and grab the first thing that passed by?

Mitch swept his hat over the fog, disrupting the blue flames and making a deep pocket that whooshed as white fire hissed out the sides to fill the hole. Mitch stood straight, leaning back so as not to get burned. His first instinct was to fan it more, but the flames died of their own accord just as fast as they had burst free.

"Not so hard," Tucker hissed. "Like this." Tucker made a rounded sweep that was more like a paddle dipping into the pool than a wave. The hole he made burned brighter, but he walked straight into it anyway. "See? Slow and easy."

"Some kinda expert you are," Mitch replied under his breath. "Been at it all of three minutes more'n me." Still, Mitch scooped at the air as Tucker had shown him and the hole it made was deep enough to see ground without bursting into flame. He shuffled forward and let the gas settle, looking for dark shadows under the surface.

Damn it if the smell wasn't worse now that everything was on fire. Smoke didn't rise from the wisps of flame that formed and vanished in the enormous pool of yellow gas, but the air smelled like a thousand matches had been lit simultaneously.

Mitch reached the wall and turned. When he looked up he saw Tucker further ahead than he expected, and what's more, he saw that the chamber wasn't just long. It turned suddenly about half the way down, back the way they had come in. He wondered if there was another passageway in there.

"Hey Tuck, do you see that?" Mitch said in a quiet speaking voice.

"The other cave?" Tucker asked. "Yeah, I see it. Catch up, will you?"

Mitch moved through the gas chamber along the wall, watching out for large shadows, but only saw one uprising stalagmite after another. It wasn't as deep along the wall so he made quick time catching up. When at last he stood across from the other cave opening his jaw dropped. About forty feet in there was what looked like a waterfall pouring gas into the pool from an open fissure in the ceiling. The sporadic blue flame butted up to ring the area where the gas tumbled into the chamber, making it look like some enchanted watering hole. He wondered how anything so beautiful could be half as dangerous as it turned out to be.

"I see a bunch of lumps in there," Tucker said with a wicked grin, blue light dancing over his dark eyes and black beard. "I think we've found our rubies."

The thought of all those rubies spurred Mitch on. He waded across the room without fanning beneath him once. Seeing the dark shadows beneath the surface in the other chamber gave him a sense of relief. He could see the difference in color of the fog, how the yellow turned almost brown around the figures beneath the surface.

"I count seven," Tucker said, pointing his pistol around the room. "That should make easy pickings between us. How about we make it interesting? First one of us to find and kill Pat gets five extra rubies from the other's share."

"You're on," Mitch said, thinking about how his share was already bigger since the numbers in the gang had diminished so. First Pat, then the Mexican, then Randy. Shoot, Mitch thought, taking in a deep, steadying breath. The last thing he wanted was to wind up like Randy.

"You go that way, then," Tucker said.

Mitch took a look in both directions. "Like hell! That's Pat over there," Mitch said, pointing the way Tucker was heading. He could tell because the size of the shadow under the surface was by far the largest of any.

"We'll flip for it, then," Tucker sighed. "Got a quarter?"

"No. You?"

"Nope. Shoot. Pick a number between one and ten."

"Why?"

"Just pick," Tucker said irritably.

"Three."

"Alright, I pick six. Closest of us to Ben's pick wins. Hey Ben!" Tucker called back out the cave opening. He didn't need to speak up too loud to be heard down here it was so deathly quiet. "Pick a number between one and ten, will ya?"

"Why?" Ben asked softly.

"Just pick," Tucker said in the same irritable tone as with Mitch.

"Five," Ben answered.

Tucker nodded his head and waved toward the other side of the cave. "You go that way."

Mitch grumbled a curse but took off his hat and fanned a trough in front of himself, taking cautious steps now that he was sneaking up on sleeping deaders. Tucker did likewise, but reached the large form of Pat Ormsby before Mitch reached the shadow a few feet ahead.

"Shoot," Tucker swore and Mitch looked his way. Tucker had a dark sneer, his black beard tilted under his angry eyes. He pointed his pistol into the pool and fired -

Blam! Mitch jerked with a start. Tucker fanned at the gas beneath him and shot again – *Blam!* "Goddamned Chinamen!" Tucker growled.

"What's going on?" Ben called out to them.

In answer, Tucker shot into the yellow pool of smoke one more time, and as he fanned at the blue tufts of fire licking the edges of the trough he'd fanned in front of him, there came a groan that rose all around them.

"What the?" Mitch whispered, looking down at the nearest shadow in the pool of gas. The big form moved, turning slowly as the yawning moans grew louder around them.

"Fellas?" Ben called.

Next to Tucker a form rose from the depths of the pool, the head of a deader, its stringy hair looking moist, pressed down over its face to hide its features. Mitch stood frozen as he watched Tucker pluck a bullet off his belt while at the same time stepping closer to the rising form of the deader. *Blam!* Mitch jumped. Tucker stepped back as the deader he'd shot slumped into the yellow pool, a burst of blue and white flame swirling around its disappearing form.

"Is that Pat there?" Tucker called over to Mitch, pointing at the large shadow slowly moving across the chamber between them. It was the one Mitch had been standing in front of. Now the form was swimming away, drawn to the loudest noise. Three more heads rose from the shadows as Tucker opened his pistol and flicked out a spent cartridge to replace it.

"I thought *you* got Pat!" Mitch yelled. The form beneath the surface stopped. Mitch's heart pounded to a halt with it. The shadow rose, breaking the surface with its large shoulders first, head hung low, thick arms dangling. "Pat," Mitch gasped. Pat Ormsby never looked so wretched. His thick neck sagged beneath rolls of loose skin, his head tilted awkwardly to one side allowing the fiery pool to illuminate an enormous purple stain covering half his face. His eyes were sunken, a vacant yearning within as he began hunting for Mitch.

"You fat son of a…" Mitch growled. Pat Ormsby moaned, taking a rigid step toward him, his arms lifting his groping hands. *Blam!* Mitch didn't flinch at the sound of his own pistol. Pat Ormsby staggered to the side from the bullet's impact.

"The head, dammit!" Tucker said hotly, snapping his own pistol's cylinder in place. "Shoot him in the head!"

Pat Ormsby steadied himself. His moan sounded hateful as he lurched toward Mitch again. Mitch raised his pistol and pointed it between Ormsby's eyes.

"Go to hell," Mitch snarled.

Blam!

Pat Ormsby's head snapped back and for a moment he didn't move at all. Mitch thought for that same second that it didn't work, that what Tucker said about shooting them in the head was a lie, but then Pat's arms began to shake as they dropped, dragging his hulking frame down with him. He sank into the yellow pool and pitched backward, churning the gas around him. The calm blue flames burst brightly and white hissing flames erupted around the falling body, burning bright and hot against Mitch's skin. He smiled with satisfaction as he held an arm up to shield his face from the sudden heat. He'd done it.

"Hey Tuck, you owe me five goddamned rubies."

Twenty-Five

Tucker lifted his pistol and shot the nearest moaner. He glared at Mitch, the gloating son of a bitch. That kind of smug got men shot in the back, but Tucker didn't have time to think about that. Two more forms rose from beneath the fissure in the ceiling, the falling gas tumbling over their heads and shoulders as they lumbered at Tucker. He side stepped toward Mitch while reaching a hand to his back, feeling for another bullet on his belt. He didn't have enough bullets loaded for all of them.

He'd counted wrong. The moaners hadn't been laying alone on the ground under the surface. Some had been two or three crowded together to look like one. Now he faced eight in all, even after the couple he'd already shot and Mitch's shooting of Pat Ormsby. *Good riddance*, Tucker thought, although he wished it was his hand that killed their ex-partner.

"You ain't won nothing yet," Tucker growled. "Get the satchel!"

Mitch nodded, stuffing his pistol in his

holster as he fanned the gas cloud with his hat around the dark shadow of Pat's body. He wasn't as scared now that the deaders were more interested in Tucker because of his shooting. Ormsby lay face up, his fat body pinning the satchel behind his back.

Just my goddamned luck, Mitch thought to himself. He stepped over Pat's body, straddling his chest with a foot on either side of his arms. He fanned aside the gas again to get a better look at Ormsby. The bullet went in just above his left eye, leaving a hole surrounded by a welt up through which a thick dark red liquid oozed. Ormsby's skin was already purplish from being dead a long time. Mitch hoped that this time it was permanent.

Mitch poked Ormsby in the chin with the brim of his hat. The fat cuss didn't stir, but Mitch jerked and reached for his gun as Tucker shot another deader, the sound of the unexpected gun blast being what frightened him.

"Shoot," Mitch hissed. He took a deep, steadying breath and fanned away the billowing yellow gas from around Ormsby again. He held his breath as he leaned down to grab the strap of the satchel, giving it a hard tug. It slid a little, but was otherwise wedged tight beneath the dead weight. He waved at the gas again, flipped his hair back with a jerk of his head, and stuffed his hat on his head so he could get both hands on the strap. He lifted straight up with all his might and Ormsby's body began to roll. He let go of the strap and took Ormsby by the arm instead, trying to roll him more to get at the satchel directly. The yellow gas crept back over Ormsby's body, rising quickly to fill the gaps. Mitch shoved his leg against Ormsby's side to keep him from slipping onto his back again, then stood up straight to avoid the rising gas.

Tucker's gun went off again just beside Mitch.

"Did you get it?" Tucker demanded, opening his pistol's cylinder to reload a few more rounds. Seven deaders were shambling toward them, all too close for them to get the satchel and escape without a gunfight.

"He's laying on it," Mitch snapped. "Help me roll him."

"Help me kill these moaners first."

"I can't," Mitch admitted, and he wasn't lying. "My leg's pinned."

"Pinned?!"

"Under Ormsby!" Mitch took off his hat and waved at the gas beneath him to show his awkward stance. He felt as though he'd topple over any moment.

"Well give me your gun, then," Tucker said, holding a hand out. Mitch glared at him, but Tucker was staring at the deaders moving ever closer. The nearest pair were holding their hands up, reaching out and yawning, their vacant moans echoing throughout the chamber. Mitch sighed and put his pistol in Tucker's hand.

"Its only got four shots," Mitch said. Tucker took two bold steps toward the gas falls while switching guns. He fired Mitch's gun at the nearest deader, hitting it in the head, then turned to shoot the next without even looking to see if the first was killed.

"Stupid idiot," Mitch mumbled while drawing his knife. He waved the gas again until he could see the ground, then reached down to start sawing the strap of the satchel. He had to put his hat on again to use both hands, and the gas seeped back over Pat's body almost as fast as he had waved it off in the first place. He listened to the gunshots as he switched between fanning the gas and cutting at the strap. After the third shot he cut through the leather strap and stood to look around, to make sure he was safe. Tucker was against the far wall with four deaders closing in on him. Mitch watched Tucker switch pistols and ready himself to shoot again.

Mitch fanned at the gas, feeling the weight of Ormsby against his leg dragging him down. He stuffed the knife into its sheath and grabbed the satchel strap, yanking it with all his might. Ormsby rolled slightly, lifting off his ankle. Mitch turned his foot, stepping over the body so both feet were on the same side, and wedged his knees into Ormsby's shoulder to get better leverage, tugging now by the big man's limp shirt sleeves. The gas filled back in and once more Mitch was forced to fan it with his hat as the snap of two more gun shots thundered through the cave.

Mitch grabbed the strap again, wrenching it free. The satchel leapt into his face, startling him, forcing him to stand straight and back up to keep balance, only his legs didn't move. Ormsby's weight settled onto his ankles and Mitch fell backwards onto his ass.

Frantically he pulled his hat off his head and began waving it around his face. He refused to breathe now that his head was beneath the surface of the pool of gas. The flames danced before his eyes, igniting into fireballs that hissed and whooshed in his ear. He stirred the gas wildly, drawing up funnels of white flame that seared his face and eyes. He kicked and squirmed to rid himself of Ormsby's weight, but the more he fought it, the more his lungs ached for air.

Just one breath, he thought. It made his lungs ache even more just thinking of it. One foot came free and for a second he swam in adulation, thanking God for seeing him to safety. In a moment he'd be free and he'd stand and breathe normally. He put his free foot on Ormsby's back to push him off as a shadow formed in the gas that roiled around his eyes.

Tucker looked down on Mitch, his black beard and hair hiding his expression. Mitch's eyes grew wide, relief and panic combining as a hundred scenarios transpired in his mind. Tucker chortled briefly and Mitch knew even before the pistol rose – that son of a bitch Tucker Adams was going to kill him with his own goddamned pistol!

Blam!

Twenty-Six

Tucker dropped Mitch's empty pistol onto the body, fanned the gas with his hat, and grabbed the satchel. He took a moment to look around and make sure there were no more moaners. As he stood over the two bodies of his ex-partners, he felt a little satisfaction for finally being rid of Mitch and Ormsby. He tucked the satchel under his armpit and poured all the empty shells out of his own pistol. He only had five bullets left, so he fanned Mitch's body again and plucked out a couple that were within reach to put in his own gun.

"Tucker?" Ben called out now that there was a lull in the shooting again. "Mitch?"

"Keep it down," Tucker said back, purposefully only loud enough that Ben would have to strain to hear. "Mitch!" he added, smirking. "Where are you? Ben is he with you?"

Tucker fanned Mitch's body again and plucked out three more bullets to put in his gun.

"What's going on?" Ben asked. Tucker almost laughed at hearing the concern in Ben's voice.

"Mitch?" Tucker said, turning and calling his name again. He closed his cylinder and moved gingerly past the bodies. "Mitch!" he hissed, trying to sound as concerned and worried as Ben had. It was easy. People wanted to be convinced. They always gave you the benefit of the doubt, especially Ben Holden. It was going to be his undoing.

"Mitch," he said again, walking across the room. Beneath the surface were the still shadows of damned near a dozen moaners. Mitch would have been a moaner soon enough, falling into the gas as he had. It was more of a mercy killing, really. No sense thinking too much about it now anyway. "Mitch?" he said one more time for show, backing out of the chamber into the main part of the cave so Ben and the woman could see him.

He stopped and looked toward the lantern light. Sure enough, Ben was standing in the pool of yellow gas up to his knees, hat off, trying to fan it to see his footing.

"Did he come out here?" Tucker asked.

"No," Ben replied.

"Damn it!" Tucker growled, shoving his pistol into his holster and making his way for Ben.

"What happened?"

"I dunno," Tucker replied, acting as

distraught as he could. "There's this waterfall – a gas fall or something – we went different ways around it. Them moaners started attacking us, and," he stopped, taking a deep breath for effect. "He found Ormsby. He got Ormsby. But he didn't get this. I had to cut it off of the son of a bitch. I thought maybe Mitch ran. He didn't come this way?"

Tucker stepped out of the pool of gas, feeling the heat drain from his legs as though he were coming out of a river. Ben came out with him, limping worse than before.

"What happened in there?"

"I told you," Tucker replied, acting offended. Ben was still trying to be leader of the gang and there wasn't even any gang left.

"We need to find him."

"Like hell. We got what we came for," Tucker said, patting the satchel in his hand. "Mitch didn't make it."

"How do you know?"

"'Cause he didn't answer when I called for him," Tucker replied irritably, walking toward Caroline. He knew where high ground in this battle would be.

"Where you going?"

"Out of here. Go on, miss, I'll lead the way."

Tucker stepped past the woman and her daughter then turned, aiming his pistol. Ben already had his hand on his own, but he wasn't fast enough. He was still giving Tucker the benefit of doubt.

"Don't even think about it," Tucker said with a wicked smile and exultation in his eyes. "You were going to shoot me in the back, weren't you?"

"Tuck," Ben said, his voice calm, trying to be reasonable. Tucker laughed out loud at him. "What's so funny?"

"You, Ben Holden. You acting like you can talk your way out of a gun fight you've already lost."

"Well," Ben said, drawing his pistol with lightning speed.

Tucker raised his pistol while squeezing the trigger, lamenting ever wasting any breath on Ben. He'd wanted to tell Ben off, to explain that all of this was his fault, first for letting Pat Ormsby ride with them, then for letting the fat cuss take the rubies, then for not catching him quickly enough, and now for all this, these moaners or deaders or whatever the hell Ben wanted to call them.

Two shots rang out and both men fell backwards.

Tucker gasped for air as he lay on his back. He'd only gotten the wind knocked out of him, he told himself. It felt like he'd been kicked hard, but he didn't feel any pain. He laughed once to himself, smiling, knowing that he'd hit Ben. He'd watched Ben fall, so he knew he'd hit him dead on. Trying to sit up made Tucker's smile vanish. The pain in the middle of his chest burst like a dam, spasms racing all the way to the tips of his fingers and toes, shaking his body violently. *Jesus!*

Twenty-Seven

Caroline hugged Suzanna to her breast, shielding her from the sight of the two men. She moved almost as quickly as the bullets, turning her daughter's head away from the violence unfolding and covering her daughter's ears. Both men hit the ground simultaneously. The man known as Tucker shook and jerked, gurgling and gasping for a moment before becoming still as death itself. The other one named Ben turned his head and looked at her, one hand covering his belly, the other holding his gun across his chest, poised in Tucker's direction. His eyes shifted to glare at Tucker, waiting for any sudden movement.

"Get his gun," Ben told her softly, his voice strong and reassuring. She had the distinct impression that this was possibly the most dangerous man she'd ever born witness to. And yet--

"What?" Caroline asked.

Ben sighed, wincing at obvious pain. "Make sure he's dead, will ya?"

Caroline sat Suzanna down and used her sign language to tell her to stay and to watch Ben. Suzanna moaned her fear and frustration, signing "don't go".

"I'm not going far," Caroline signed back. She kissed her daughter's forehead, signing that momma would be fine, and managed to free herself of her girl. She stood and took a deep breath, gripping the axe in both hands as she approached the sprawled out form of Tucker. A dark stain had grown over his chest. She didn't bother looking where the bullet had struck. It was too gruesome, even with everything she'd already seen. Instead, she looked at his eyes, still as stones. She turned the axe over and let the handle slip in her hands. The blade slid toward the ground, landing in Tucker's crotch hard. Tucker didn't even flinch.

"He's dead," Caroline said aloud, mostly for her own reassurance.

"So it seems," Ben replied, swallowing the lump in his throat.

Letting go of the axe handle, Caroline crouched down and slipped the pistol from Tucker's limp fingers, backing away as quickly as she could.

"The satchel," Ben said to her. She held the pistol as it was intended and approached Tucker again, grabbing one of the cut straps of the satchel and hauling it free of Tucker's death grip. Tucker's arm fell limply and Ben sighed again, this time in relief.

"You've used a gun before?" Ben asked and Caroline nodded. "Good. Now take your girl and get out of here."

"What?"

"I wasn't walking good before the bullet in my belly," Ben said. "I don't think I can make it out of here on foot."

"Well that's just stupid," Caroline admonished. She signed for Suzanna to take the satchel as she handed it to her daughter. Caroline walked around Ben and knelt down beside him. "You only have to make it as far as the rail cart," she told him.

Ben brightened at the thought, a single laugh escaping. A smile lifted one side of his rough face. "Help me up," he grunted, stuffing his pistol into its holster.

Caroline swept his arm around her neck and steadied herself. He was much heavier than most men. Ben's burly arm felt hard against the back of her neck, his muscles taught as he began to rise. He let out a cry of pain even as his teeth bore down to grind away the protest plaguing his body. Caroline planted her feet to stop him from pitching over.

"Can you walk?" she asked, already breathless. She slid Tucker's pistol into a large pocket on her dress, handle first.

"I'll need help," Ben replied, using her

as a crutch for his bad leg.

As they passed Suzanna, Caroline signed for her to stay close, guiding her around Tucker's body while at the same time trying to keep herself and Ben blocking the girl's sight of the body. Each step came with a softer grunt as Ben grew accustomed to the new kind of pain tormenting his body. The fire in his stomach tore at his right side each time he set his weight on the ground, as though he were ripping the muscles by stretching them too far. It was the bullet wound, he knew.

They hobbled down the passage slowly. Each time the girl tried to get past Ben he'd hold his free hand out to keep her back. The girl tried on Caroline's side with the same gentle admonishments, which made the orange glow of the lantern light stretch wildly along the walls. The trick of light he'd seen going up didn't appear ahead of them as they rounded the corner. Ben looked back to see a ring of blue light circling the cave edge, much brighter than the soft glow of green covering the walls.

Good riddance, he thought, and not just about the eerie pool of glowing gas they were leaving behind. He was glad his fight with Tucker had finally come and gone. Waiting to be shot in the back was something that had been weighing on him for months. Thinking of it helped calm the sharp spikes running through his back with each step, but even so he had to stop to rest twice before they reached the large cave with all of the passages.

Caroline helped him to the passage leading out. He kicked his own silver dollar he'd left on the ground as he passed it by, feeling better about trusting the woman. She was a good woman, he reasoned. The cave was too narrow for two abreast, making them walk sideways, Caroline in front hauling him up each irregularly spaced step. It was much easier going up than down because of the angle of the cut outs, but his whole body wanted to collapse every step of the way. He could feel himself dragging her down.

"A few more steps," she kept insisting. Ben wasn't sure if she meant for him to try just a few more, or that there were only a few more left. The girl had gotten ahead of them in the big cave and now stood facing them three steps ahead, the lantern in front of her, watching her mother with worry. Each time they got close enough to reach out and touch her she spun around and rushed ahead to wait…just a few more steps. Just out of reach.

Then the girl ran ahead and disappeared. Caroline called out her name in a worried tone, but even Ben knew it was no good. The girl had reached the cavern with the rail cart and had gone inside ahead of them.

"Go get her," Ben grunted, trying to shift his weight away from Caroline to lean against the cave wall. In the darkness left behind by the girl's departure, Caroline couldn't see Ben's eyes, nor could he see hers. Only the outline of her face beneath her tangled hair was there. She let him go and rushed up the last few steps, her form a black shadow rising into the orange glow lost somewhere ahead. Then she, too, disappeared.

The darkness felt alive with the gentle breeze from below whispering in his ears. He dug in his pocket for the box of matches. In the same pocket were two broken candles. Falling after being shot had snapped them in half, but they were still linked together by string and hard to tug out. He struck a match and cupped his hand around it as best he could with a candle between his fingers. The breeze threatened to put out the hissing flame. He coaxed it to the wick and held his breath. The flame caught and he sighed, turning the light of the candle to see ahead, still shielding the flame with his other hand.

He knew he was in bad shape. His back and legs still ached unreasonably, threatening to reach the limits of his tolerance with each step. Even now, as still as he tried to be, the weight of his body was like a hundred sacks of stone pressing down on nails into his lower back. The thing that worried him, though, was the fiery lances that came from his stomach every time he flexed or stretched the wrong way. He held the candle low to his shirt to get a better look. There wasn't much blood, which was good. It meant he didn't need to hold a hand over it constantly, but he needed some bandages or something tied around his waist. Maybe he could cut off some of the woman's dress, he thought. Where was she?

He hobbled forward. He could hear her voice in the chamber ahead, her tone soothing and soft. Her words were too quiet for him to hear, though. He reached the step and managed to swing his good leg up without inciting the pain in his belly. Lifting himself up the step sent a wave of agony to his knees and he caught his breath in surprise. He let his breath out when the pain subsided. He wouldn't be able to get out of these mines alone on foot that was for sure.

Still, he managed the last two steps and leaned against the cavern entrance with his candle flickering and dying in the sudden change of direction in the breeze. The air circled the room before rushing off in different directions, making it hell on an exposed flame.

The rail cart was in the middle of the room, his salvation. Beyond it, kneeling down in front of her daughter, was Caroline. She cupped her daughter's head in her hands and was singing softly, swaying back and forth. When the girl looked toward Ben, Caroline said "It's all right. Watch my lips. Sing with me."

Ben waited. The girl didn't look back at her mother. "Ma'am," Ben said, interrupting her quiet song.

Caroline didn't budge, though her singing ceased. "Why won't this end?"

"It will," Ben said. He hoped his tone was reassuring. The pain he suffered made it hard to believe even himself. "Help me into the rail cart."

Caroline signed something to her daughter before coming to Ben's side. He waved out the candle and stuffed it back into his pocket. Using her for support they reached the rail cart quickly. He steadied himself against its frame for a moment.

"You'll have to help me in," he said, turning around to face her. "Lift my legs."

"Hang on to the brake," Caroline instructed. Ben grabbed hold of the wooden handle she pointed at. She knelt down and tugged on a metal bar under the cart. The metal sang out a creaking, grinding chirp and the edge of the cart Ben was leaning on began to rock freely under his weight.

"What are you doing?" Ben asked.

"I'm going to dump it out," Caroline grunted as she put her shoulder to the edge and tried to turn the cart. It creaked and pitched sideways, the rubble and rocks inside the cart tumbling to the other side, helping her in her efforts. She stood up straight and lifted the bottom of the cart, spilling the rock and debris with a crumbling hiss.

"Get in," she said. Ben hobbled to the side of the cart and knelt down. The pain tore through his back. He fell forward into the bucket of the rail cart. Caroline must have let go because his legs were lifted off the ground and he tumbled into the bottom of the bucket head first. The pain stabbed him in a hundred places and he cried out, cursing a stream of words as he hauled himself in further and rolled to a sitting position. The bucket still swayed as he sat still, panting like a dog, waiting for the agony to subside.

There was another grinding of metal and the cart became rigid as stone again. Caroline stood up and looked in on Ben. She didn't apologize. Instead, she tried pushing the rail cart. It began to roll and Ben felt a new wave of relief wash over him. The cart stopped as Caroline turned back toward her daughter.

"Come on, Suzanna," Caroline said, signing something with her hands. The girl rushed over to her mother's side and Caroline once again started pushing the rail cart. Ben could see her face in the glow of the lantern. She was straining with all her strength to move him. The cart began to roll again and he held his breath, worried that if he started to have hope, something bad might happen. He turned his head, craning his neck to look ahead toward the darkness of the way out.

Twenty-Eight

The passage wasn't steep, thank goodness, but there was an incline, and the woman simply didn't have the strength to push the cart far. She leaned against the brake handle to catch her breath. The girl stood along the side of the passage, holding the lantern and satchel and watching her mother. After catching her breath Caroline put her back to the cart, thinking that a different way of pushing it might make it easier getting up the rise.

Ben remained silent. He wished there was some way of helping her, but he couldn't climb out now even if he tried, and he had been dumped in on the wrong side of the cart to be able to hold the brake for her when she needed to rest. Making matters worse, every time he tried to shift positions he was seized with tortuous spasms of pain.

"It's only a few more feet," she breathed, her head low as she pushed a third time, once again facing the cart. The wheels of the cart rolled slowly, grinding out every inch with the crack and snap of grit being crushed between the iron wheels and tracks.

"It levels out ahead," Caroline said as she leaned against the brake again. "It'll be easier from there. Just a few more feet."

Ben didn't say a thing, afraid that he might interrupt the spell she wove for herself. He lay a hand over the wound in his stomach where an oozing of blood had soaked through his shirt and vest. It still wasn't bleeding badly, but he wished he had something to bandage it.

Craning his neck over the edge of the cart to see ahead of them all he saw was the orange light fading into darkness as the passageway rose and slowly curved. The long stretch of shadows played tricks on his eyes. Everything moved, but he couldn't hear anything over the chirping and grinding of the wheels. It radiated up through the iron bucket, drowning out his other senses.

"What was that?" Ben hissed, unsure if he'd seen the reflective flash of an eye, or just some trick of the lantern light on a crystal or moisture in the wall. Caroline ratcheted the brake and looked up, breathless.

"What?" she whispered.

"I thought I saw something," Ben replied, trying to crane his neck further.

Caroline squinted to see into the darkness. "I don't see anything," she whispered.

Ben looked back at her and then into

the tunnel they had come up. He could no longer see the room from which they had started. The passage appeared far steeper than he'd realized.

"Why don't you rest a spell," Ben said.

"No." Caroline shook her head. "It's just a little farther. A few more steps."

"Ma'am," Ben said, thinking to argue the point. She bent forward again and started pushing, the slow trundling of the wheels echoing through the cavern. Ben looked over toward the girl. She stood still, staring at her mother who was struggling to save him. The cart moved ahead so slowly that the girl only took a few steps to keep up before Caroline stopped again, breathless.

"Ma'am."

"I said no," she snapped, looking up with determination in her eyes. Her gaze didn't linger on him. She looked past him toward the darkness, her eyes widening with terror.

Ben craned his neck. Lurching out of the long shadow cast by the curve of the passageway were three figures.

"Dear God," she breathed, horror stricken.

Ben drew his pistol and tried to roll on his side. Pain raged down his spine, seizing his legs in a sudden spasm that shook him head to toe. His uncontrolled jerk doubled the pain he suffered and he cried out, dropping his pistol into the cart. The metal clanked and rattled beneath him.

Caroline ushered her daughter to her side, waving frantically. She couldn't leave the rail cart without letting go of the brake. Suzanna rushed to her mother's side and with one arm Caroline tried to shield her daughter from the sight. The lantern swung in her daughter's hand, stretching and shrinking black shadows on the cavern walls. The figures looked like apparitions as they lurched ever closer to the rail cart.

Ben felt for his pistol, biting off the pain.

"What do we do?" Caroline whispered.

Ben had plenty of ideas, but running away again didn't seem like a good one. Not when they were so close to getting out. His hand closed on the pistol beneath him and he held it up for Caroline to see. She shook her head, pulled her daughter to the side of the cart, and began to let the brake go. The cart creaked as it rolled slowly back into the mine.

"No," Ben hissed and Caroline plied the brake again. "I can kill them," he said, waving his gun.

"If you shoot them and they fall across the tracks, who's gonna clear the way?"

A moan rose in the cavern before he

could answer, followed by another. Ben craned his neck and aimed at the nearest figure, a lean man wearing just a stained white shirt with one arm sleeve rolled up. The deader was still too far away for a good shot.

"No," Caroline roared. Ben turned to see her reaching a hand toward her daughter. The girl was rushing toward the deader, her own little arms outstretched as though seeking an embrace. Ben felt the rail cart begin to move as the woman leapt forward in an effort to grab her daughter by the arm sleeve. Caroline had to take several steps to catch up to her girl, and in that time the rail cart sank away, rolling down the passageway into darkness.

Ben could see Caroline look back in his direction, tugging on her daughter as she tried to retreat to the rail cart, but the thing accelerated quickly. At first he thought she might have had a chance, but like a train picking up steam out of a station, the cart continued to gain momentum, leaving her and the girl behind.

It was a brief ride. The cart swept down a slope that left the glow of the lantern behind. Ben turned to look ahead, but it was pitch black, and although the air pushed against him like a mild breeze, he knew by the sound of the rolling wheels he was moving fast. Despite his pain he lunged forward, hoping to find the brake handle where he thought it to be. His hand caught emptiness and the pain in his body burned as if he were lit on fire. In another second he felt weightless. His legs struck something solid and he felt himself spinning. His gun went off. In the momentary flash he saw the rail cart upside down behind him. The sight vanished with a thud as something heavy struck him in the back of the head, and even though there was darkness he saw white light everywhere for a moment, then all was silent, his pain vanished, and as he recognized that he no longer felt pain, even that notion vanished into blackness.

Twenty-Nine

Caroline led her daughter down the passageway after the rail cart, leaving the shambling figure of her husband and the other dead townsfolk behind. Her grip on Suzanna was fierce, tight as a vice. She was furious with her daughter for breaking free like that. They had talked about it already. She had told Suzanna that the man that looked like Daddy was a monster.

She heard a crash echoing up the passageway. The rail cart must have hit the bumper, she realized. She hoped the man called Ben was alright, but the decision she had made was the only one in her mind. Letting go of the brake was the only way to save her daughter.

"Come on," Caroline told her daughter, tugging at her. The girl couldn't run fast enough, and thankfully she couldn't hear the bitterness of Caroline's words either. Caroline slowed, tugging a little more gently, realizing she was on the verge of hysteria. "Come on," she whispered, looking down at her daughter with kinder eyes. "We'll be fine," she signed with her free hand, letting Suzanna's arm free and taking the satchel to hold her daughter by the hand instead. She gave Suzanna's hand a gentle, loving squeeze.

In the cave at the bottom of the sloped passage they found the rail cart still standing, but turned sideways and off of its tracks. Beyond the upright stop posts Caroline saw the man lying on the ground in a heap of twisted limbs where he had been thrown. She slowed, not willing to bring Suzanna any closer.

"Mister," Caroline called out. "Mister, are you alive?"

There was no response, not even a groan of agony.

Jesus, what was she to do with a man's body if he were still alive anyway? She couldn't very well stand over him and shoot every last one of the dead sure to come through here.

"Mister," she shouted, hoping he might still be alive, praying that he wasn't.

"Come on," Caroline said, signing to her daughter, leading her down again, deeper into the mine. Going out the main mine entrance wasn't an option anymore. She knew she couldn't shoot her way through the oncoming dead even with a hundred bullets. She didn't have the strength to shoot her own husband in front of her daughter. Alone, maybe, but with Suzanna watching…

At the entrance to the passageway leading down she stopped.

"Mister?" she asked one last time, looking back toward the unmoving jumble of limbs. Her voice was soft. She didn't want an answer.

Down they went, taking the steps as quickly as she could make her daughter move. She wanted to be far ahead of the dead. The light of their lantern would draw them if they could see it. The steps seemed endless even though she knew there were hardly a hundred of them.

"Come on," she whispered to her daughter needlessly. "Just a few more steps."

She reached the room with several passages and went straight to the one she knew was the other way out. On the ground there was a candle, the one she'd seen that man throw here earlier as a way of finding it if something happened. She kicked it aside and stepped around it out of a superstitious feeling that he was somehow still linked to it.

Thirty feet in, the passage started to fill with rubble and debris that slowly rose into a wall. At the top of the pile of boulders and rocks was a rift torn out of the ceiling that lead upward at an angle.

"Come on, Suzanna," she said, signing

to climb in front of her. Her daughter handed the lantern to her mother and began climbing the stones on all fours. Caroline tied the cut strap of the satchel around her waist like a belt and started climbing up after her daughter. She wondered if there really were rubies in it.

Thirty

At dawn Caroline watched the line of dead march in rigid ranks up the hillside and into the darkness of the mines. Suzanna had slept on the ground all night, curled in her dress, her head in Caroline's lap as her mother watched the hole in the hillside they had come out of. She watched the mine entrance and the hillside in every direction. Caroline had waited for that man to emerge, expecting the echo of gunshots and his fiery eyes filled with a rage and determination to hunt her down. She knew he didn't have bullets enough to fend off the horde descending upon him if he had survived the few stragglers that had gone in throughout the night. If he wasn't already dead, he soon would be. Whether they tore him apart or he became one of them she didn't care anymore. To her, they were one and the same now.

With the dead back underground, she woke her daughter and stretched her legs, slapping the dust from her dress. She had a plan – to get as far from town as possible by nightfall. She hoped there were still canteens in the store. It was forty miles to Bishop to the

East. She didn't want to head toward Fort Brennan and run into the townsfolk again.

They walked down the hillside toward town, Caroline still holding her daughter's hand. Suzanna had pulled through the worst of things fairly well. In the next several days, Caroline knew she would need to talk with her daughter, tell her things would be all right, that what happened won't ever happen again, and that those were the only monsters in the world.

"Come on," Caroline whispered. "Just a little further."

They reached town and stood at the end nearest the stables. Caroline expected more of the dead to rise up around her at any moment. She was afraid to go into the general store to look for supplies for the walk ahead of them. Yet the town was deserted except for several dead bodies lying in the street. Buzzards were already staking their claim, their black wings outstretched to guard their prize.

"Ma'am?!" came a surprised voice. Caroline started and turned toward the stables. Up in the loft one of the gang of men was lying on his belly with a rifle tucked under his arms. "Ma'am, where'd you come from?"

Caroline only pointed toward the hillside.

"Are they all gone?" he asked and she nodded, wondering if he meant the other outlaws, or the dead.

The young man, a kid really by the looks of him, backed out of sight and she could hear him climbing down the ladder of the loft. It was so quiet in town. Suzanna looked at the young man approaching and then looked at her mother. Caroline stared at him with a leery gaze.

"Are you all right?" she asked, noticing his limp.

"I should ask you the same," the kid said with a wide grin. "You two look like hell. Holy geez! You've got the satchel," he said, dropping the rifle and hobbling around behind her to look at the pouch. "Are they in there?" he asked excitedly.

"Why are you limping?" Caroline asked him.

"Oh, it ain't much," the young man said with a wave, hobbling back around in front of Caroline, still grinning ear to ear. "One of them moaners bit my foot. Burns a little when I step on it. Two of them did it, actually. You wouldn't believe what happened."

Caroline signed for her daughter to turn around as she fished the pistol from her pocket. It felt heavy in her hand as she lifted it and pointed it at the young man. He'd been bitten and soon he'd turn into one of the dead. He may as well be dead, she thought. This was a favor she was doing for him even though it would haunt her the rest of her days.

"Ma'am, what are you doing?" he asked.

"I'm sorry," she said, gulping at a lump in her throat. She squeezed the trigger.

It was the loudest gun blast she'd ever heard. It shook her head to toe. Her hands trembled and she dropped the gun, fighting away tears as she stepped beside her daughter to shield her from the sight and to lead her to the store.

"Come on," Caroline whispered. "Just a little further."

The End

23797419R00118

Made in the USA
Charleston, SC
02 November 2013